MY LiFe
as a
Beat-Up
Basketball
Backboard

the incredible worlds of **Wally McDoogle**

MY LiFe
as a
Beat-Up
Basketball
Backboard

BILL MYERS

NELSON®

Thomas Nelson, Inc.

Nashville

Published in Nashville, Tennessee, by Tommy Nelson®, a division of
Thomas Nelson, Inc. Visit us on the web at www.tommynelson.com

Scripture quotation is from the HOLY BIBLE, New International
Version (NIV). Copyright © 1973, 1978, 1984 International Bible Society.

Library of Congress Cataloging-in-Publication Data

Myers, Bill, 1953–
    My life as a beat-up basketball backboard/ Bill Myers.
        p. cm.—(The incredible worlds of Wally McDoogle; #18)
    Summary: Misadventures abound when the Ricko Slicko Adver-
tising Agency arranges popularity and fame for clumsy Wally
McDoogle, young writer of superhero stories.
    ISBN 0-8499-4027-3
    [1. Popularity—Fiction. 2. Self-acceptance—Fiction. 3. Authorship—
Fiction. 4. Christian life—Fiction. 5. Humorous stories.] I. Title
PZ7.M98234 My 2000
[Fic]—dc21   00-025058
                                                              CIP

Printed in the United States of America

06 07 RRD 13

For Carl and David . . .

Thanks for the neat title, guys!

"Before I formed you in the womb I knew you, before you were born I set you apart."

—Jeremiah 1:5 (NIV)

Contents

1. Just for Starters . . .   1
2. A Day in the Life of . . .   14
3. On the Ball (or under it . . .)   23
4. Rockin' and Rollin'   36
5. The Fame Game   46
6. Willard Weirdness   59
7. Reality Pays a Visit   69
8. Blame the Fame   81
9. Let the Game Begin   92
10. Wrapping Up   104

Chapter 1

Just for Starters . . .

All right, all right . . . maybe wanting to be the most popular kid in the world was a bit of a stretch. Still, I do have a certain reputation. Need somebody to trip over his shoelaces and fall flat on his face every time he gets in front of the class? I'm your man. Need someone for the eighth graders to turn upside down, stick his head into the toilet, and flush? Here I am.

So, when Ricko Slicko's Advertising Agency claimed they were so good that they could take the biggest loser in the country and turn him into the most popular guy on the planet, I knew I qualified. Quickly, I fired off a letter to them saying that they *had* to pick me. Unfortunately, every kid I knew fired off a similar letter. This might have made the competition a little tough except for one minor detail . . . all their letters recommended me, too!

Now Ricko Slicko himself was downstairs talking with Mom and Dad to see if I really was the world's biggest klutz, while I was upstairs in my bedroom praying hard that I would be chosen:

Please, God, I'll do anything You want. You want me to empty the cat box for life? Done. You want me to change my socks more than once a week? Deal. You want me to eat my little sister's cooking without coughing, gagging, and calling 911? Um, er, can I get back to You on that?

"Wally? Will you come down here a moment?" It was Mom! I could tell from her voice that a decision had been made.

All right! Great! And I didn't even have to agree to eat my sister's cooking!

But she wasn't finished. "I'm afraid we've got some disappointing news for you."

Okay God, how 'bout if I just eat the stuff that hasn't been charcoal-ized?

I finished the prayer and quickly opened my door. A simple task for most human beings. Unfortunately, I'd forgotten the part about moving my head out of the way. (Hey, I can't remember everything.)

K-FWAMP
K-THUD
shatter, shatter, shatter

The *K-FWAMP* was the hard door hitting my soft nose.

The *K-THUD* was that same hard door hitting my glasses.

And the *shatter, shatter, shatter* was the lenses to those glasses cracking into a hundred pieces, which would explain the hundred versions of the world I now saw, which would also explain . . .

"WHOA!"

not seeing my sister's Barbie convertible sports car when I staggered into the hallway. No problem—except for the part where I stepped into the toy's front seat, couldn't get my foot out, and began to

roll, roll, roll, roll

down the hall. It's not that I couldn't remove my foot; it's just that I wasn't sure which one of the hundred feet below was my real foot.

Even that wouldn't have been so bad, if it wasn't for our cat, Collision, who, as you may recall, did not get his name by accident. At the moment, he was sitting on a table beside the giant aquarium at the end of the hall next to the steps. He was staring at Dad's tropical fish, obviously dreaming of sushi, when *roll, roll, roll, roll*

"LOOK OUT!" I cried. "COLLISION, LOOK OUT!"

K-RASH
"MEOWRRRRR!"
glug, glug, glug, glug

In sheer terror he sort of attached himself to my chest. Meanwhile, the aquarium toppled over, turning our stairway into a miniature water park—complete with five tropical fish and one boy shooting the rapids with his foot stuck in a Barbie sports car.

After watching my life pass before my eyes (scary all by itself) and telling God I'd even eat my sister's charcoal-style cooking, I finally

K-"Ouch!"

hit the bottom of the stairs.

As far as crashes went, it wasn't bad. On the McDoogle Scale of Mishaps, it only registered a 6.8, which explains why Mom and Dad weren't too concerned. (It's only when I break through the wall and into the neighbor's house that they start to get nervous.)

"Wally," Dad calmly said as he helped me to my feet, "I'd like you to meet Mr. Slicko of Ricko Slicko's Advertising Agency and his Lovely Assistant, Doris."

As I stood, I did my best to pry Collision off my chest. Finally, he released his claws and

MEOWRRR . . .

went flying across the room. Well, actually not "across the room," more like directly on top of Lovely Assistant Doris's head.

She screamed and hollered, then did a little dance. Collision howled and dug his claws in a little deeper . . . which made her dance a little harder . . . which made Collision howl even louder and dig his claws in even . . . well, you get the picture.

Meanwhile, I did my best to appear calm and collected as I tried to shake Mr. Slicko's hand. (I would have appeared more calm and collected had I known which one of the hundred hands reaching to me was his.)

"Hello, Willard," he said.

"Maff's Mwally," I answered. It was supposed to be, "That's Wally," but for some mysterious reason I was speaking a foreign language. Fortun- ately, the mystery didn't last long as my Barbiepowered foot suddenly shot out from under me, causing me to crash to the floor and spit out Dad's prized Zanzibari sunfish.

And there, staring down at my soaked and battered body, was Lovely Assistant Doris, who danced and screamed . . .

as Collision howled and hissed . . .

as five exotic fish flipped and flopped . . .

as the last of the water trickled down the stairs. Ricko Slicko turned to my parents.

"Mr. and Mrs. McDorkel," he said, beaming, "I've changed my mind. Your boy is *exactly* what we're looking for."

* * * * *

That night, I was so excited I couldn't sleep. Think of it: Me, Wally-the-Walking-Disaster-Area McDoogle, becoming the most popular guy in the world. Was such a thing possible? Granted, people had been convinced that Pokémon cards were actually worth trading, but to get people to believe that I was actually popular? What's next? Convincing them that a book with a character named Harry Potter could actually sell? Was there no end to the miracles that could be accomplished?

To help pass the time, I reached for Ol' Betsy,

my laptop computer. Maybe writing one of my superhero stories would help me unwind. I opened the screen, punched on the power, and went to work . . .

Our superhero, the ever-popular and always-careful-to-brush-between-meals ImaginMan, looks out his spacecraft window. To his surprise he sees a giant flock of meteors flying straight for him. Before he has a chance to ask if meteors really fly in flocks (or do they travel in herds or schools, and if it's schools does that mean they go through different grades until they graduate—and more important, who cares?) he fires his retrorockets to dodge those rascally rocks.

He dodges to the left. They're still coming.

He dodges to the right. And still they're coming.

In a flash of heroic thinking our hero heroically thinks: *Uh-oh, I'm dead!*

Suddenly, he recalls his newly installed Meteor Eater (sold at Inter-galactic department stores everywhere).

With one flick of the switch he releases a powerful spray that covers the deadly rocks and immediately turns them into Jell-O pudding (your choice of chocolate or vanilla).

"Oh, boy!" he shouts as he reaches for a bowl and spoon. "Dessert!"

The blobs of pudding splatter against the front of the ship as ImaginMan sends out his trusted robot, R-2 M-NOT, to scrape off the delectable delicacies and bring them in.

Then, just when you'd think things couldn't get any weirder

BRR-ING

the phone on his desk rings. The only problem is,

BRR-ING,

his spaceship doesn't have a desk. Come to think of it,

BRR-ING,

it doesn't have a telephone, either.

Suddenly, he remembers he's reading a book. That's right, it is merely his finely tuned imagination (along with some incredible writing on this author's part) that made him feel he was dodging meteors and eating pudding.

BRR-ING

He slams the book shut and races to the phone to beat the fourth ring, before that pesky answering machine kicks in.

"Hello?" he says.

"ImaginMan, is that you?"

ImaginMan strains to listen, but it's hard to hear over all the

BLEEPS, PINGS, and BLAMS

going on in the background.

"Who is this?" he shouts.

"The Vice President of the United States."

BLEEP, PING, BLAM

"Sir, I can barely hear you. What's

going on? What's all that noise?"

"It's horrible!" the Vice President
cries. "It's hideous! It's horrendous!
It's—"

"I get the picture," our hero inter-
rupts.

"Are you sure? 'Cause I got a few more
'H' words. How 'bout horrific or—"

"Sir, where are you?"

"I'm hiding under the President's
desk."

"Why?"

"That awful alien from the planet
Brain Freeze is trying to take over the
world again."

"You don't mean—"

"That's right, it's that villainously
vile villain . . . (insert scary music
here) . . . KidVid! He's on the loose and
he's got a brand-new plan."

BLEEP, BLEEP, BLEEP

"What is it this time, sir?"

"He's passing out free computer games
to everyone in our world."

PING, PING, PING

"I don't understand. How's that a problem?"

"Soon everyone on Earth will become so addicted to these mindless games that his planet will invade ours without a fight."

BLAM, BLAM, BLAM

"What's going on in the background?"

"Our beloved . . . President"—the Vice President's voice grows weaker—"they've already . . . got him . . . hooked."

"You mean on the game?"

"Yes! I'm the only one left." His voice grows more and more faint. "Can . . . no longer . . . resist."

"Sir," our hero shouts, "you've got to hang on!"

"Must . . . play . . . game."

"Mr. Vice President! Don't give in to its power! Don't give in!"

But it is too late. Now the only thing our hero hears over the phone is

BLEEP, BLEEP, BLEEP
PING, PING, PING
BLAM, BLAM, BLAM

and background voices speaking
in dreaded Videoese: "Cool, dude . . .
awesome shot . . ."

Quicker than you can ask yourself,
"Hey, is Wally picking on video games?"
our hero races to his front door,
throws it open, and runs out into the
street.

It's worse than he suspects. The
streets are deserted. No one is working, no one is shopping, no one is
going to school. Everyone has called
in sick and is staying home, glued to
their TV screens and computers. All our
hero hears through the open windows are
mindless grunts and groans, accompa-
nied by even more mindless comments.

It's terrible, unbelievable, almost
as bad as watching professional
wrestling. (Well, not quite, but you
get the drift.) And it's all the work
of (more scary music, please) KidVid!

ImaginMan must act fast. It's time to
do what he has to do, so he better
hurry and do it.

Translation: It wouldn't hurt to get
                a move on.

He spins around, races back into his house where he slips into his ImaginCape, then enters his ImaginCave where his ImaginMobile is idling, waiting for him to hop in, when suddenly—

"Wally! Wally, are you in bed?"

I looked up from Ol' Betsy a little startled. "Yes, Mom," I called out. "I'm sound asleep."

"Nice try, son. Now get to bed; tomorrow's a big day."

"Okay," I called.

I shut Ol' Betsy down and snapped off my bedroom light. I suspected that the only thing as weird as my ImaginMan story would be what I would face tomorrow—what I would have to do to become the most popular kid in the world.

Unfortunately, I couldn't have been more wrong. Tomorrow wouldn't be as weird as my superhero story, it would be weirder. A lot weirder.

Chapter 2

A Day in the Life of . . .

"Willard, wake up now. Wake up."
I quietly rolled over, . . .
gently yawned, . . .
slowly opened my eyes, and . . .
LEAPED OUT OF BED SCREAMING FOR MY
LIFE

"AUGHHHHH!"

My room was packed tighter than Aunt Thelma's
girdle. At least a half-dozen strangers were cram-
med inside, with twice that many TV lights blaz-
ing away. And every eye, every light was focused
upon yours truly.

Now, being someone who always keeps his cool,
especially in unusual situations, I calmly opened
my mouth and, at the top of my lungs, shrieked,

"WHAT ARE YOU DOING IN MY ROOM?!"

"Relax," a familiar voice called from behind me, "everything's okay."

I twirled around to see Ricko Slicko by a cameraman who was videotaping my every move. "This is going out LIVE to fifty million households across the nation," he said.

"It is?" I gave an embarrassed little smile.

"That's right." He grinned.

Instantly, I did what any self-respecting person appearing in fifty million households would do . . . I looked down to make sure the front of my pj's was buttoned.

Good. Now on to less important issues. "W-w-what's going on?" I stammered.

"It's all part of my campaign," Mr. Slicko replied. "It's a new TV show called *A Day in the Life of Willard McDorkel*."

"That's 'Wally McDoogle,'" I corrected.

"Whatever. The point is, you've got an entire nation watching you this very moment. Now is the time to impress them all."

I turned back to the camera, once again feeling my mouth twist into a self-conscious grin.

"Is there anything you'd like to say to them?" he asked.

"Me?" I kinda croaked.

"That's right, Willard. Is there anything you'd like to say to more than fifty million people? This is your big chance."

My heart pounded. My mind raced. He was right, this was my big moment. All I had to do was say something clever, something brilliant, something that would make me the most popular person in the country. But what? What could I possibly say to impress an entire nation?

"Well?" Mr. Slicko asked, motioning for the cameraman to move in for a nice, tight closeup.

Finally, I had it. Something incredibly profound, something deeply important. "I just want to take this opportunity to say . . ."

"Yes," he said, coaxing me on with an encouraging grin. "Don't be shy."

"Well . . ."

"Go ahead, Willard."

"I have to go to the bathroom."

* * * * *

It took a little doing, but I finally convinced them to let me go into the bathroom alone (though I wouldn't be surprised if they got some good sound effects of the toilet flushing). Anyway, when I stepped back into the room, the TV crew was still standing there taping.

Normally, I get dressed before going downstairs to eat breakfast. Call me shy, but for some reason I didn't feel like stripping in front of fifty million households. Then there was the matter of my *Star Wars* underwear. (Hey, at least I got rid of those Barney ones.)

So, instead of changing clothes, I decided to head downstairs first. And, even though I walked into the kitchen several minutes earlier than normal, my entire family was up and waiting.

"Oh, Wallace," Mom said, cranking up a perma-grin smile for the camera. "You brought your friends. What a surprise." (The fact that she was wearing her best evening gown and already had been to the beauty parlor made me wonder exactly how surprised she really was.) "Here, dear, sweet, wonderful son, let me pour that breakfast cereal in the bowl for you."

At first, I thought she was laying it on a bit thick, until my older twin brothers, Burt and Brock, got into the act.

"Hey, Wally," Burt said, while carefully flexing his biceps for all the babes out in TV land to see, "let me pour some milk on that cereal for you."

"Hey, Wally," Brock said, while carefully pulling his hair down in his eyes for that sexy movie-star look, "let me lift that heavy old spoon up to your mouth for you."

Needless to say, it was weird to have my older brothers make such a fuss over me. (Normally, I'm lucky if they even remember my name.) But that was nothing compared to the kindness and consideration of my little sister, Carrie.

"Guess what, Wally?" she said, scooting up beside me and batting her baby blues at the TV camera.

"What?" I asked.

"I've decided not to cook for a whole month."

Wow! Talk about thoughtful! Talk about caring! Was there no end to their kindness?

And then, topping it off, there was Dad. To be fair, the guy really isn't much of a morning person. In fact, on a good day we're lucky to get a grunt out of him. But today . . . well, today he actually looked up from his morning paper and spoke. It really wasn't much, but for Dad it was like the Gettysburg Address . . .

"Mornin'," he grumbled.

Talk about a miracle! For a moment we all stared at him in speechless awe. And then, doing our best to appear as the perfect, loving family, we gave the perfect, loving answer in perfect, loving unison:

"Good morning, Father Dear."

Talk about perfection. Talk about the ideal family. Talk about making your stomach turn.

The rest of the breakfast went pretty well . . .

except for the part of my spilling milk (twice), accidentally tipping over the cereal bowl (three times), and trying to head back upstairs (which I fell down more times than I could count).

"All right," Mr. Slicko groaned on my fifth—or was it my seventh?— fall. "We'd better go to commercial. Go to commercial, NOW!"

Lovely Assistant Doris spoke into her headset, and they turned off the lights and camera.

"So, how am I doing?" I asked, looking up from the bottom of the stairs.

He shook his head. "We've got to think up another angle. We're trying to make you the most popular kid in the world, not the most pathetic."

"Hey"—I shrugged as I struggled back to my feet—"you said you wanted somebody who was a klutz."

"Yes," he replied, nodding, "you've certainly not disappointed us in that department. Listen, during the commercial break, go upstairs and get ready for school. We'll meet you outside on the porch. By then I'll figure out some way to make you look like a hero."

And, believe it or not, that's exactly what he did . . .

Ten minutes later, as I stepped onto the front porch, the TV lights blazed on and the camera began rolling.

"All right," Mr. Slicko whispered into his walkie-talkie. "Signal the driver."

Before I even started down the steps, a flashy red convertible squealed around the corner. It swerved back and forth, wildly out of control. As it approached, I could see the driver. He was a man made up to look like an old woman—complete with a very bad-fitting dress and an even worse-fitting wig. "Help me! Oh, help me!" he/she screamed. "Oh, my! Oh, my! Who can possibly save me?"

"Okay, Willard," Mr. Slicko whispered.

"That's Wally," I whispered back.

"Whatever. The point is, that's your cue. Get out there and save her!"

All I could do was stare at him. Don't get me wrong: I have nothing against saving little old ladies in runaway sports cars (even if they happen to be men), but I also have this thing about wanting to live . . . I was about to point this out to Mr. Slicko when suddenly another person burst out of the bushes beside me. And if that wasn't weird enough, he looked exactly like me! It was amazing—the same shirt and pants, the same blond hair, and, of course, the same nerdy glasses.

Poor guy.

I was going to tell him how sorry I was about his appearance, or at least write him a nice sympathy card, but it didn't look like he had the time. Instead, he raced across the lawn and right out into the street.

"Oh, my! Oh, my! Is that the great Willard McDorkel?" the pretend man/woman screamed from the car.

"Yes," the photocopy version of me shouted. "Do not fear, it is I!"

And then, before anybody could pass out awards for the world's worst acting, Photocopy Boy leaped onto the passing car, crawled into the driver's seat, and brought the vehicle to a screeching halt.

"Oh, Willard! Oh, Willard! You have saved my life!" the man/woman in the wig cried. "How can I ever repay you?"

"No problem," Photocopy Boy answered. "It's all in a day's work. Now, if you'll excuse me, I have to stop a runaway freight train before heading off to school."

"And cut!" Mr. Slicko cried. "Great, let's go to another commercial."

The TV lights went off and the crew began to applaud. Soon, both actors climbed out of the car and gave polite little bows.

"Nice work, Willard." Mr. Slicko turned to me, grinning. "Soon, you'll be everyone's hero."

"But . . . ," I sputtered, "that wasn't me."

"Exactly. That was your stunt double. From now on, he'll be doing all your dangerous stunts."

"You mean like walking up the stairs without falling down, or chewing gum without spraining my jaw?"

"Yes," he said, nodding, "but that's just for starters. Soon you'll be pulling people out of burning buildings, saving passengers from sinking ocean liners, and convincing mothers not to fix fried liver—even when it's on sale."

"But I can't do that kind of stuff!" I objected.

"Of course *you* can't, but your stunt double can." Mr. Slicko flashed me another grin, the one I was liking less and less. "And that will be our little secret. Only you and the TV crew will know the real truth."

I frowned. "But . . ."

"Listen, do you want to be popular or not?"

"Yes, of course I do."

"Then just leave everything to me."

I swallowed hard and nodded. Already I suspected things were going to get a little worse before they got better. Unfortunately, I should have suspected that my suspecting was a little suspicious.

Translation: Things were *not* going to get a little
              worse . . . they were going to get *a lot*
              worse.

"Actually, what I need," she said, "is your official endorsement of this." She dug into her backpack and pulled out a four-inch plastic doll with blond hair and cracked glasses. One that looked strangely familiar.

"Don't tell me," I said.

"That's right," she said with a grin. "It's the new Crash 'n Burn Wally action figure."

"Oh, brother," I groaned.

"No, listen," she said. "You just wind it up like this." She gave it a quick wind. "Set it down on the ground, like this." She set it down on the floor. "And step back," she said as she released the little toy. In 1.3 seconds it ran into the nearest wall and exploded into a giant fireball.

"Cool?" she asked, waving the smoke out of her face.

I coughed and answered, "Maybe a little extreme for the younger crowd."

"Not if they've read your books."

I had to nod. When she's right, she's right. "What's my take?" I asked.

"The usual. I get one hundred percent of the profit, and I give you a whole zero percent."

In case you forgot, Wall Street's whole purpose in life is to make her first million by the time she's fourteen. And so far she'd been making most of it off me. So, without a moment's hesitation, I

stuck out my hand, shook hers, and cried, "Deal!"
(Hey, I'm a writer, not a businessman.)

"McDoogle! Get your rear in here!" It was the
delicate voice of Coach Kilroy bellowing from
the gym.

"On my way!" I shouted. "Gotta go," I said to
Wall Street.

She nodded. "Oh, and Wally?"

I turned back to her.

"If you should die while becoming famous . . ."

"Yes?" I said, waiting for some thoughtful, sensitive last word.

"Can I have first dibs on your toenail clippings?"

"Sure," I said. "What are friends for."

"McDoogle!"

"Coming!"

* * * * *

I'm not entirely sure why Coach Kilroy had
such a grudge against me. It might have something to do with my last misadventure—the one
where I got him thrown into jail and nearly
destroyed the world in the process. (I tell you,
some people can be so touchy sometimes.) Anyway,
somehow Mr. Slicko managed to talk Coach into
letting me practice with our school's basketball
team, the Middletown Clams. Some teams have

tigers or bears or eagles for their mascots. We've got clams. Don't ask me why, just lucky I guess. And don't even get me started on those two guys who have to dress up like clamshell halves every game.

Anyhow, in a matter of minutes I was suited up and out on the floor with the guys. It was pretty exciting and, of course, majorly painful. I'll save you all the gory details and just cut to the headlines. First, we had the world-famous:

LAY-UP DRILLS
A piece of cake. Someone passes you the ball, you leap into the air, and slam-dunk it into the basket. No problem—well, except for the part of catching the ball, leaping into the air, and slam-dunking it. Actually, I didn't even get as far as the leaping and dunking. I was still working on the catching.

K-THWACK
K-FALL
K-unconscious

The *K-THWACK* was the ball bouncing off my chest at supersonic speed.

"Come on, McDoogle," Coach Kilroy shouted. "You're supposed to catch the thing!"

The *K-FALL* was me staggering under the impact of the ball, which would lead us to the third and most important sound effect . . . *K-unconscious* (which really isn't a sound effect at all, but me cracking my head on the floor and suddenly deciding to pass out).

"Come on, McDoogle, this is no time to rest! Quit slacking! Get on your feet! Be a man!"

Actually, *being a man* was the least of my priorities. Right now, all I wanted to do was *be alive* . . . until Coach dragged me over to the next drill, which was:

DRIBBLE DRILLS

"Okay men," Coach barked. "I want you to dribble the ball fifty times with your right hand, then fifty with your left, then fifty with your right, then fifty with your left."

No problem. Anybody could do that. (Well maybe anybody else's body, but not this body.)

K-DROP! bounce . . . bounce . . . bounce

"No, McDoogle! You don't drop the ball. You slam it down hard enough to make it bounce back up!"

"Oh, right." I giggled nervously. I picked up the ball and tried again. This time I threw it down as hard as I could.

of applause, please), but forgot to move my face out of the way when it came back up. This, of course, would explain the

K-RACK

rebreaking of my glasses, not to mention the

K-LATTER, K-LATTER, K-LATTER,

which is the sound your front teeth make when they are knocked out and fall onto a basketball court.

"McDOOGLE!"

"Sorrwy," I mumbled, "dwidn't meam dood." I dropped to my knees and scooped my teeth into the container my orthodontist had given me for just such occasions.

And finally, what basketball practice would be complete without the ever-popular and even more painful:

STAIR DRILL

This is where you run up and down the three flights of stairs inside the school.

"To build up those leg muscles and teach you endurance!" Coach Kilroy shouted. Of course, in my case, it was to wheeze my lungs out and teach me more humiliation.

K-SLAM

It was an impressive display of strength, I was pretty pleased . . . well, except for the ṛ where it hit my foot

K-BOING

bounced wildly off to the side and

K-RASH

hit the fire alarm, which

RINGGGGGGGGGGGGGGGGGGGGGGGGG . . .

went off.

Which, of course, set Coach Kilroy off. "McDOOGLE!"

Naturally, we all had to traipse outside and stand in the freezing rain until the fire department came to tell us it was okay to go back inside, which probably explains why nobody was too concerned when we returned to the drill and I

K-BOUNCE

slammed the ball down, missing my foot (a round

The wheezing my lungs out, you can understand. It's not that I'm in bad shape, it's just that
I work up a sweat brushing my teeth. (Hey, those
toothbrushes can get heavy.)

Then, of course, there was the matter of my
humiliation. It wasn't the twenty minutes it took
to get up to the top of those three flights that was
rough. It was when I got to that last step, my foot
slipped, and I tumbled backward that things got
a little embarrassing.

Even that wouldn't have been so bad if the rest
of the team wasn't behind me on their fiftieth or
sixtieth lap. Somehow, I managed to hit all of
them, sending us tumbling down the three stories
of stairs until we landed in a giant, tangled heap
at the very bottom.

It was a beautiful feat of clumsiness . . . one
human bowling ball knocking down an entire team
of human bowling pins. A perfect strike in every
sense of the word. But apparently Coach wasn't
much of a bowling fan:

"Get away from my boys!" he screamed. "Get
away from my team! Get away from my gym! Get
out! Get out! Get out!"

As someone with above-average communication
skills, it was my impression that Coach didn't
exactly want me around. So, taking the subtle
hint, I dragged my beaten and battered body to

the showers. I had no idea how painful becoming popular could be.

I got out, toweled off, and dressed. I pushed open the door and had barely stepped outside before I ran into Mr. Slicko, who was waiting for me with the rest of the TV crew. This time, however, there were some additional people:

"Willard? Willard McDorkel?"

I turned to see three girls running toward me. They were about my age, maybe a little younger. One was on a pair of crutches.

"Would you please sign this?" Girl One asked breathlessly as she shoved a piece of paper at me.

"What for?" I said.

"What for?" she asked. She turned to her friends and sighed dreamily. "He asked what for."

The second girl spoke, her voice sounding even mushier than the first. "Not only is he courageous, he is *sooo* humble."

"And even more gorgeous in person than on TV," Girl Three sighed as she shoved up her glasses and shifted her weight on her crutches.

"TV?" I asked.

"Oh, yes," Girl One said, nodding enthusiastically. "We saw the way you saved that poor woman's life this morning in the runaway car."

"It was so cool," Girl Two said.

"And dreamy," Girl Three sighed.

"That's right," Girl Three replied as she fondly ooked into my eyes.

"Why would you do that?" I asked.

More giggles all around until she answered. "Because that's what *you* do, silly."

"Well, yeah, but I'm . . . I'm a natural klutz. I don't do it on purpose. I just sort of—"

"Show him your glasses," Girl Two said.

Girl Three took off her glasses and poked her fingers through where the lenses were supposed to be.

"I . . . don't understand," I said.

She batted her eyes some more and explained. "Unfortunately, my eyes aren't as bad as yours, so I can't wear real glasses like you. But that doesn't stop me from getting to wear the frames."

"You *want* to wear glasses?" I asked.

"You bet."

"And the reason you want to wear them is?"

"Because you do, silly."

Another round of giggles.

Once again, I felt that strange combination of greatness and uneasiness. But before I had a chance to sort it out, a giant stretch limo squealed around the corner and pulled up beside us.

"Great," Mr. Slicko called from behind the camera. "Your limo's here. Come on, Willard, we've got to get going!"

I threw a nervous glance over at Mr. \
was giving me a thumbs-up sign. I cl\
throat. "Well, actually, you see, the pe⟩
stopped the car really wasn't—"

"And after you've given her your autograₚ
you sign my wrist?" Girl Two asked as she s.
her hand in front of me.

"And my leg cast," Girl Three said, blinking
eyes at me faster than a strobe light.

Finally, I was starting to get it. "Well, sure,\
said. It was hard not to smile as I grabbed a peₗ
and reached for the first girl's paper. It felt a little
strange that someone would actually want my
autograph. But it also felt kinda good.

"Oh, thank you, thank you." Girl One sighed as
I finished signing her paper. "I will treasure this
always."

"Oh, thank you, thank you," Girl Two said as I
finished signing her wrist. "I will never wash my
hand again."

"Oh, thank you, thank you," Girl Three said as I
finished signing her cast. "I will never take this off."

My smile kept growing. I couldn't help it. It was
finally happening. I was finally getting popular.
"So tell me," I asked the girl with the cast, "what
happened to your leg?"

"She threw herself down the stairs," Girl One
explained.

I looked up, surprised. "Where to now?"

"To the rock concert," he said.

"Rock concert?" I asked. "We're going to a rock concert?"

"That's right."

"Whose?"

"Yours, of course."

If I was surprised before, I was downright astonished now. This was incredible. First working out with the basketball team, then signing autographs for my fans, and now taking off in a limo to star in my own rock show.

"This is great," I said as we climbed into the car.

"I figured you'd like it, Willard."

"You keep calling me that, but my name is Wally, remember? Wally McDoogle."

He frowned. "No, that name is too goofy. Sounds like a hero in some kid's comedy book series."

"Well, actually, now that you mention it—"

He cut me off. "I like Willard better. Willard McDorkel. Yeah, that's got a nice ring to it." Then, slapping me on the back, he grinned. "Looks like you can kiss the old Wally McDoogle good-bye, son. I'm turning you into someone entirely different. I'm turning you into somebody worshiped and adored by millions. Wally McDoogle is history. Now there's only Willard . . . Willard McDorkel, superstar!"

Chapter 4

Rockin' and Rollin'

"AND NOW, LADIES AND GENTLEMEN . . . MEN . . . MEN," the announcer's voice echoed through the packed auditorium.

I stood backstage waiting to go on. As I waited, I nervously adjusted my bald wig. Earlier, when we were in the dressing room putting it on, I had asked Mr. Slicko why I had to wear it.

"It makes you look like a punker," he explained.

I shook my head, causing all my fake earrings, fake nose rings, and any other fake body piercings to clang into each other. All the jewelry seemed a bit extreme but, hey, if that's what it takes to be famous, it was worth it, right? Still, I thought the bald wig was a little much. "This isn't what I look like," I said. "I'm no punker."

"Oh, I know that and you know that"—Mr. Slicko gave me a little wink—"but your new fans out in the audience don't."

I was getting that uneasy feeling again, but I wasn't sure why.

Once they had put the bald wig on, the next thing were the tattoos (also fake). Fake serpent heads, fake skull and crossbones, fake bloody daggers. You name it—if it was in bad taste, they put it on me.

"But this stuff is all so creepy," I complained. "I don't like it."

"Of course you don't. But if you want to be popular and famous, you've got to pretend you do."

"But it's not me."

"That's the whole point, Willard. If you want to be famous, you gotta be somebody else."

"But I like who I am."

Mr. Slicko arched an eyebrow. "You're kidding, right?"

"No, I do," I insisted. "Well, kinda."

"Fine. If you want to be you, then you'll have a fan club of one. But if you really want to be popular, if you really want to be famous, then you've got to be who *they* want you to be."

Before I could argue, he'd shoved a lit cigarette into my mouth. "And make sure you keep this in the whole time you're onstage."

"But—" That's all I got out before I accidentally breathed, which caused me to accidentally cough a lung out, then turn green, then throw up. (No wonder smoking is bad for your health.)

"Hmm," Mr. Slicko said as I continued my coughing, gagging, and dying routine. "Might be better if you don't inhale."

That had been half an hour ago. Now I stood backstage all made up, with a guitar around my neck, a cigarette in my mouth, and more graffiti on my body than the wall of an inner city.

All this as the announcer continued his introduction:

"AND HERE'S THE MOMENT YOU'VE ALL BEEN WAITING FOR . . . FOR . . . FOR. LIVE AND IN PERSON . . . SON . . . SON, WILLARD McDORKEL . . . ORKEL . . . ORKEL."

The audience went crazy.

"Get out there!" Mr. Slicko yelled. "Your fans are waiting!" He gave me a shove and suddenly . . . I was onstage. The lights were blinding, the audience was screaming, and I was . . . well, once again, I was beginning to think that it might all be worth it. I mean, let's face it, there's something pretty exciting about having ten thousand fans screaming . . . especially when they're all screaming for you.

Things were going great until I took that second step onstage.

K-twist
K-PLOP

Apparently, I wasn't so great at walking in platform shoes. No problem. I scrambled back to my feet, took another step and

K-twist
K-PLOP

gave a repeat performance.

Once again I got up, and once again . . . well, you get the picture.

The embarrassment continued as I slowly made my way across the stage.

K-twist
K-PLOP
K-twist
K-PLOP

Unfortunately, it wasn't too long before I noticed that all of the cheering and screaming had come to a stop. Now there was only silence. Dead silence. (Well, except for the sound of blood racing to my cheeks and ears as I experienced major humiliation.)

I turned to the band members that Mr. Slicko had hired to accompany me.

Their mouths hung open as they stared at me in utter disbelief.

I turned to the audience. Through the glaring lights I could make out enough faces in the first few rows to see . . . their mouths hanging open as they stared at me in utter disbelief.

Uh-oh. It was over. I could tell. As I lay there sprawled out on the stage in front of ten thousand staring fans, I knew I'd been found out. With any luck I could sort of just crawl off the stage and disappear. Maybe I could change my name (again). Maybe move someplace where I was less known. (I hear Antarctica is beautiful this time of year.)

And then, suddenly, I heard a noise over by the band.

K-PLOP

I turned to see my lead guitarist throw himself down onto the floor.

What on earth?

He began playing as he leaped up and did it again, this time along with my keyboard player. Then again, with the bass guitarist getting into the act. Before I knew it, the entire band was throwing themselves down on the ground and getting back up, then throwing themselves down and getting back up. (All in perfect rhythm to the music.)

I could only stare, more clueless than usual when, out in the auditorium, I heard . . .

K-PLOP, K-PLOP
K-PLOP, K-PLOP, K-PLOP.

I turned and looked out to the audience. I couldn't believe my eyes (or ears).

K-PLOP, K-PLOP, K-PLOP
K-PLOP
K-PLOP, K-PLOP
K-PLOP, K-PLOP, K-PLOP, K-PLOP

All over the auditorium people were standing up and throwing themselves down on the ground. Then standing up and throwing themselves on the ground—in perfect rhythm to the music. I looked on, completely amazed. It was incredible. Astonishing. Someway, somehow, I had accidentally started a whole new fad . . . a brand-new dance craze.

K-PLOP, K-PLOP
K-PLOP, K-PLOP, K-PLOP, K-PLOP

I turned back to Mr. Slicko, who was giving me not one, but two, big thumbs-up. His face was cranked up into a major this-is-going-even-better-than-I-had-planned grin.

The music continued—loud and blasting. Even though I was supposed to be the lead singer I had

no idea what to sing. But it didn't seem to matter.
The entire audience was too busy screaming
and throwing themselves down on the ground to
notice. Oh, sure, I'd yell something every so often—
while trying to stand and

> *K-PLOP*
> > *K-PLOP*
> > > *K-PLOP.*

But, other than that, there wasn't much I
needed to do . . . except realize that Ricko
Slicko's plan was once again succeeding.

* * * * *

I'd just stepped out of the limo and started
toward my house when I heard a familiar voice.
"Hey, Wally?"

I turned and there was Wall Street approaching. Beside her was my other best friend, Opera.
(That's Opera as in overweight Italian singers.)

"Did you see my concert?" I asked.

"Yeah." Wall Street nodded.

I turned to Opera, who also nodded and answered, *"Crunch, crunch, crunch."* Besides classi-
cal music Opera has this thing about junk food. He
loves it. The guy is crazy about any kind of chip.

And it doesn't matter what type . . . potato, corn, poker; if it ends in "chip," he'll eat it.

"So what did you think?" I asked. "I tell you, nothing beats having ten thousand fans screaming for you."

"We gotta talk," Wall Street said. "I've got to ask you a question."

"Munch, munch, munch," Opera agreed.

"I know." I smiled kindly as I reached into my pocket for a pen. "You want my autograph, too, don't you?"

"What?" Wall Street frowned.

"Burp?" Opera scowled.

"My autograph," I said.

"Get real," Wall Street scoffed.

"Belch," Opera agreed.

"We just want to know what you think you're proving!" Wall Street demanded.

"About what?" I asked.

"About pretending to be someone you're not."

I grinned. "Pretty cool, isn't it?"

"No, it's not cool," Wall Street said. "Actually, it's pretty pathetic."

"What are you talking about?"

"I'm talking about all this fake body piercing, all these fake tattoos. And what's with that cigarette you were pretending to smoke?"

Her tone bugged me, but I figured it was just

jealousy (and who could blame her). I tried to stay calm. "It's just part of my new image," I explained.

"New image?"

"That's right. For people to like me, I gotta act the way they want me to act."

"What about the way *we* want you to act?" Wall Street asked.

"Burp," Opera agreed.

"Sorry, guys." I gave my head a little shake, causing my earrings to jangle. "I guess this is just the new me."

"But we don't like the new you," Wall Street argued. "It's just not . . . you."

I was getting tired of all this complaining. Didn't she know who she was talking to? Didn't she see me save that car on TV this morning? Didn't she see me up onstage? "If you don't like the new me," I suddenly heard myself say (a lot creepier than I wanted to), "then maybe you should go find a new friend."

"Crunch, munch?" Opera looked up at me in surprise.

"You heard me." The words came out faster than I could stop them. "I've got thousands of new friends who like me just the way I am."

"Munch, crunch?"

"That's right. In fact, they worship the ground

I walk on. So if you don't like the new me, I've got ten thousand other people who do."

"Make that nine thousand nine hundred ninety-nine," Wall Street said. "Come on, Opera, let's get out of here. This sidewalk isn't big enough for us and Wally's ego."

"That's Willard!" I heard myself shout. "Willard McDorkel!"

Without another word they turned and started heading down the street. I couldn't believe my eyes. Didn't they know who they were walking away from?

"Go ahead!" I shouted. "I've still got nine thousand nine hundred ninety-nine friends!"

That was when Opera looked over his shoulder and shouted back, *"BELCH!"* (Which translated means, "Make that nine thousand nine hundred ninety-eight!")

I thought of yelling something else, but it didn't matter. Hey, I was popular now. I didn't need them. I was famous. I didn't need to hang with a bunch of losers. Sure, I had to give up little bits and pieces of myself along the way. Sure, I had to pretend to be something I wasn't. But it seemed a small price to pay to finally have my dream come true.

Little did I realize that my dream was about to become a nightmare . . .

Chapter 5

The Fame Game

It had been quite a day and I was glad to get to bed. But my brain was still reeling with all the cool stuff that had happened—and with all the uncool stuff Wall Street had said. So I decided to unwind a little by getting back to my superhero story.

I grabbed Ol' Betsy, punched her on, and went to work . . .

When we last left our incredibly intense and intelligent ImaginMan . . . (I'd include information involving his impossibly industrious and idiosyncratic ingenuity, but that's too many "i's," let alone words I don't understand and that you'd just skip over anyway, so why bother.)

Where was I?

Oh yeah. Our hero has just slipped on his ImaginCape, entered his ImaginCave, and has raced off in his ImaginMobile. (Any similarity to another superhero is strictly coincidental—especially if he happens to be wearing a pointed black mask and is named after a flying rodent.)

But where to begin? How can ImaginMan hope to find the awesomely awful and astonishingly awkward alien? (And you thought I could only do that with "i's," didn't you?)

The last time that creepy KidVid tried to take over the world it was by making everyone watch *Teletubbies*, then it was *Barney* reruns, and don't even get me started on those *Brady Bunch* marathons. But now, trying to destroy everyone's brain cells by making them play video games nonstop? Is there no end to his dubiously diabolical dastardliness? (Or am I trying to wear out your mouth with these tongue twisters?)

In a flash of inspiration, ImaginMan reaches down and snaps on his Bad Guy Detecto Screen (sold at Good Guy Gadget

stores everywhere). Carefully, he begins
scanning the area for KidVid's spacecraft when, suddenly—

BLEEP, PING, BLAM

his Bad Guy Detecto Screen is filled
with weird-looking creatures blasting
away at even weirder-looking creatures. No, this is not some Power
Rangers rerun; it's KidVid's new video
game!

Great garbanzo beans! He's striking
everywhere! Not only that, but our hero
suddenly discovers a set of controls
that have been conveniently placed on
the seat beside him. He picks them up,
and before he knows it, he begins
pressing the buttons . . .

BLEEP, BLEEP, BLEEP
PING, PING, PING
BLAM, BLAM, BLAM

"Hey," he shouts, "this is kind of
fun!"

Oh, no! Even ImaginMan is getting
hooked! Now he is staring mindlessly at

the screen while mindlessly pressing
buttons, and having a mindlessly good
time.

"No, ImaginMan," the incredibly handsome
writer of this story types. "Stop playing! You
have to resist its power!"

Our hero glances up from the screen.
"Who said that?"

"It's me, Wally McDoogle, your author."

But unimpressed, he turns back to
the screen as the dull, vacant look
returns to his eyes.

Quickly I type: "You can't be conquered
by KidVid."

"Why not?" he mumbles while mindlessly pressing the buttons.

"Why not?" I write.

"Why not?" he repeats.

"Why not!"

"I think we got the question covered,"
he mutters. "How 'bout an answer?"

Suddenly, I have it and I quickly type, "Because
you're supposed to prove to the world
how great it is to use your imagination!"

"Imagination?" he asks.

"Yeah, you know, like reading and
stuff like that."

But ImaginMan barely hears. He is too
busy

BLEEP, PING, BLAMming
BLAM, PING, BLEEPing

"Besides," I type, "you can't be driving your ImaginMobile and playing
video games at the same time."
"Why not?" he mumbles.
"'Cause if you don't pay attention
to your driving, you're going to hit
the semitruck I'm adding to the
story."
"What semitruck?"
"The one that's completely out of
control, racing toward you at a hundred miles an hour, and

HOOOOONK . . .

blasting its horn."
Our hero looks up from the game just
in time to see the truck. He slams on
his brakes. He grabs the steering wheel
and yanks it sharply to the right,
missing the passing semi by inches.

After spinning out of control, he finally screeches to a stop.

"Wow," he gasps, "that was close! How'd you do that?"

"I just used my imagination," I type. "The same imagination you use whenever you read."

"Pretty cool," he says.

"You bet," I type. "Now, can we get on with the story?"

"You're the one with the imagination; let's do it!"

With that our hero leaps out of his car. He will no longer use his Bad Guy Detecto Screen for fear of again getting hooked on the video game (even though he almost had enough points to go to the next level). Instead, he searches the skies for any sign of KidVid's spacecraft.

There is nothing above except a few clouds and the passing Good Ear Blimp— the passing Good Ear Blimp that now has a video screen on its side playing . . . you guessed it

BLEEP, PING, BLAM

KidVid's video game! And, as our hero
stares, he once again begins falling
under its spell.

"No, ImaginMan!"

"Must . . . find . . . controls," he mumbles.

"No! ImaginMan, you have to resist!
You have to fight this thing!" I type.

"Must . . . go to . . . next . . . level."

"No, ImaginMan! No!"

But it is no use, ImaginMan's imagination is once again turning to mush.

Oh, no! What will he do? If he falls
under KidVid's spell, how can he possibly help others? Doesn't he realize
the fate of the entire world rests in
his hands? More important, doesn't he
realize that my superhero stories never
end this early in these books?

I paused for a moment, staring at Ol' Betsy.
KidVid was having a lot more of an effect upon
our hero than I had imagined. And for some
strange reason, the more I thought of KidVid's
power, the more I thought of Ricko Slicko's . . .

* * * * *

Don't ask me why, but the next day Coach Kilroy let me back into practice. Maybe it had something to do with the new team uniforms appearing on his doorstep. Or the brand-new glass backboards that were installed overnight. Or maybe it was connected to the money a secret donor contributed for a new gymnasium—complete with workout room, swimming pool, and a special sauna just for coaches. A secret donor whose first name began with the letters R-I-C-K-O and whose last name ended with the letters S-L-I-C-K-O.

Still, if I thought yesterday's workout was tough, it was nothing compared to the scrimmage Coach had us running today. We'd barely begun, and already I was so beat that I was sucking up more air than a Hoover vacuum cleaner.

And why not? I'd run up and down the court three whole times. And now, for some reason, Coach Kilroy wanted me to do it again!

"Get back down here and guard your man, McDoogle! Defense, defense, defense!"

"But I was just there!" I cried, wheezing and coughing up major body parts.

"Get down here!" he yelled.

"But they'll just shoot another basket *(cough, cough)* and come back here *(gag, gag)*!"

"That's the idea of the game!" he shouted.

"Well, it's a dumb idea!"

"McDOOGLE!"

"All right, I'm coming, I'm coming."

Translation: "All right, I'm dying, I'm dying."

Now, I'm no rocket scientist, but it would seem a lot easier if we'd just stay at one end of the court and let their team make all the baskets they want . . . then stroll on down to our end and shoot till we were done. Talk about a great way to make friends. And think of the wear and tear we'd save on our tennis shoes (not to mention our bodies)!

Better yet, maybe we could decide the winner by sitting around and playing a heated game of rock, paper, scissors.

I was about to make these brilliant suggestions to Coach Kilroy when suddenly I noticed the ball coming directly at me. Can you imagine that? Someone had actually passed *me* the ball. Someone had actually expected *me* to do something with it.

Now it was time for me to do what I do best. Now it was time to demonstrate my incredible athletic ability. Now it was time to drop to the ground and let that puppy sail right over my head.

ZWINGGG . . .

"McDOOGLE!" Ah, yes, the delicate, caring voice of Coach Kilroy. "This ain't dodge ball. You're supposed to catch the thing!"

"Ohhhh," I said, scrambling to my feet and suddenly understanding. "You mean like yesterday?"

"NO!" He shook his head in panicked concern. "Not like yesterday! I don't want any more broken teeth, or broken glasses, or ringing fire alarms."

I frowned. "What's left?"

"Just put your hands out and catch the ball."

"Really?"

"Really," he sighed.

"All right, if you say so."

It was a pretty weird concept, but I thought I'd give it a try. The next time the ball accidentally came my way I put out my hands, and

ZWINGGG . . .

it went straight through them.

"McDOOGLE!"

"It didn't work, Coach."

"You're supposed to close your hands when it reaches them!"

I tell you, the man was a genius. No wonder they made him coach. And thanks to his detailed instruction I was now fully prepared. The next time a teammate decided to trust me and pass the ball (sometime around the year 2047), I not only stuck out my hands, but I actually closed them around it. And you know what?

I caught it!

Talk about exciting. Talk about amazing. Talk about making it into *Ripley's Believe It or Not!* One guy from the other team was so excited that he raced up and started waving his hands in my face. He was obviously as thrilled as I was. Wanting to share my joy (and realizing they'd probably put the ball on display at the Smithsonian Institution), I decided to let him hold the glorious object for just a moment.

"McDOOGLE!!"

"What now?"

"You're not supposed to give the ball away, you're supposed to keep it!"

I groaned. "This game's got too many rules!"

Well, as you probably guessed, for the rest of the scrimmage my team did everything they could not to throw me the ball. But as luck would have it, with ten seconds left—after it was dropped, batted, and bounced past everyone else—it just sort of rolled to a stop at my feet.

It was time to be the hero and prove what I was really made of. With a sudden burst of Olympian prowess, I reached down, picked up the ball, and did not give it away!

"Go, McDoogle!" Coach shouted. "You've got eight seconds, go for it!"

I looked up and saw him motioning me down the court. This was too good to be true. At last, I could make up for my mistakes. At last, I could make Coach proud of me.

"Six seconds, McDoogle! What are you waiting for? GO!"

I nodded, stuck the ball under one arm, put out the other, and began running down the court.

"No, McDoogle!"

In my head I could hear the play-by-play commentary. *He's at the forty-yard line, folks. The thirty-five, the thirty!*

"McDoogle, you've got the wrong sport!"

I knew Coach was shouting something, but it was hard to hear over my imagined crowd and screaming announcer. I guess he'd just have to wait until the post-game show to talk to me.

He's at the twenty, the fifteen . . . I spotted a member from the other team coming at me. But that was no problem, I simply sidestepped him, spun to my left, faked to my right, and continued my sprint to the goal line.

The ten, the five . . . TOUCHDOWN WALLY McDOOGLE!

In my head, the fans were going crazy. I could picture my agent demanding fifteen million dollars to renew my contract. While, all the time, in the distance, I could hear Coach Kilroy screaming: "Get him off my court! Get him off! Get him off! Get him off!"

Poor guy. He was so overcome with pride for teaching me the game that he could barely talk.

"Please . . ." He broke down, sobbing like a baby. "Just get him out of my sight . . . please."

I'd have loved to stick around. Maybe pass out a few autographs to fellow team members, or hang out with Coach to receive the key to the city. But I could see Mr. Slicko and his crew standing outside the doors waving for me to hurry and join them. Great. I could hardly wait to discover what exciting adventure into popularity he had planned for me next.

Chapter 6

Willard Weirdness

"So what are we doing here?" I asked as our limo pulled up to 2½ Flags Amusement Park. (They wanted to be Six Flags, but it wasn't big enough.)

"Watch and be amazed, Willard," Ricko said. "Watch and be amazed."

Three minutes later the TV crew and I were strolling through the park. To our left was Space Molehill (it would have been Space Mountain, but I already mentioned the size problem), which, of course, would explain The Pirates of the Wading Pool ride to my right. Up ahead was It's a Small, Small, I'm Talking Microscopically Small, World.

And then I saw it . . .

My mouth dropped open, my eyes grew wide, and my heart pounded louder than a bad rap song. Because there, rising before us, was a giant head. It was at least six stories high. A roller coaster raced into its mouth and, by the yelling and screaming that echoed inside, it was obvious the passengers were having the scare of their lives.

But it wasn't the size of the head or the screaming inside that had taken my breath away. It was what the head looked like. Or should I say *who* it looked like. It had blond hair, black-rimmed glasses (shattered, of course), and an expression of total cluelessness.

I began to stutter, "It's . . . it's . . . it's . . ."

"That's right, Willard, it's you."

"You had them build a ride about me?"

"Yup. And according to the park officials, it's the hottest ride in the park."

Suddenly, a roller coaster raced out of the left ear, wound around the jaw, and came to a stop directly in front of us. But instead of getting up to leave, the passengers, who seemed to be coated in some sort of slime, just sat there with dazed expressions. Some tried to speak, but instead of words all that came out was

"Ma-ma-ma-ma . . ."

They were definitely shaken. In fact, the ride had taken so much out of them that assistants had to help their trembling bodies from the roller coaster and carefully guide them toward the exit.

"Come on," Mr. Slicko said, pulling me to the

front of the line. "Let's see what all the excitement is about!"

"Hey, no cuts!" a big bruiser of a kid shouted.

Mr. Slicko turned back to him and calmly asked, "Don't you know who I'm with?"

"I don't care who you're—" That's all Big Bruiser got out before he saw me. "It's not possible," he gasped. "It's . . . it's . . . Wilfred!"

"That's Willard," Mr. Slicko corrected.

Word spread up and down the line like wildfire. Before I knew it, everyone was swarming around me.

"I'm so terribly sorry," Big Bruiser pleaded. "It was my mistake. Please, cut in front of me."

"No," a pretty girl shouted, "I want him to cut in front of me!"

"No, me!" another begged.

Things were getting pretty rowdy (not to mention crowded) as they continued to surround me. In fact, it was all the park assistants could do to pull us from the line and escort us to the next waiting roller coaster.

"Thanks," I said while catching my breath and taking a seat in the front.

"No prob," an assistant said with a grin. "Now be sure to buckle in nice and tight."

"Why's that?" I asked.

He flashed what almost looked like a sinister

smile. "In the next three minutes and forty-five seconds you'll be reliving every one of Willard McDorkel's mishaps."

I gulped nervously. "Every one?"

"Well, not every one," he said, "just the high-lights, which, as you and I know"—he lowered his voice so as not to frighten the other passengers—"isn't a pretty sight."

Then, with a menacing chuckle that grew to an ominous laugh, he released the brake . . . and we were off!

We shot into the giant mouth and entered what looked like a river in the woods. I immediately recognized the scenery of Camp Wahkah Wahkah from *My Life As a Smashed Burrito with Extra Hot Sauce.* For the most part it looked pretty realistic. Even the upcoming waterfall.

Upcoming waterfall!

That's right. Before I knew it our car was

"Augh!"

shooting off the top of a waterfall and tumbling straight down. Yes, sir, it was just like old times. The same life passing before my eyes, the same praying to God to forgive me for everything I'd ever done wrong, and the same promise that if

He let me live I'd quit making those stupid jokes about my sister's cooking.

But instead of hitting the pool of water below, we were suddenly caught in midair by the mouth of a mechanical creature that looked exactly like the one from *My Life As Alien Monster Bait*. I let out my breath, I started to relax, I told God I was probably still going to make those stupid jokes, when suddenly the mouth opened and we were once again

"AUGH!"

falling.

This time, however, we landed in a giant hot-air balloon basket like the one from *My Life As a Broken Bungee Cord*. That was the good news. But, as we all know, for me there's always some bad . . . Our roller-coaster car was too heavy and the entire balloon started falling toward the earth. Well, actually not the earth, more like a jungle river. No problem except for the giant reptiles that were swimming below waiting to turn us into crocodile junk food.

Listen, God, I know I keep going back and forth about those jokes, but I really will quit making them if You'll just—

K-CHLINK

That, of course, is the sound of a roller-coaster car landing safely on top of the head of a giant dinosaur skeleton (complete with giant dental floss hanging from its mouth). Whew, that was close.

Where was I? Oh yeah. *But God, they really can be funny, and her cooking really is awf—*

Unfortunately, my negotiations were interrupted by a couple more sound effects. Like the

RATTLE, RATTLE, RATTLE

sound of dinosaur bones falling all over a museum floor, and the sound of me

"Augh!"

screaming as we headed toward that same floor at a thousand miles an hour.

I'll save you the gory details. Let's just say that the ride went on and on . . . and then on some more. Before I knew it, we had become torpedo test targets, then human hockey pucks, then big-foot breath mints. It was awful, terrible, worse than Dad keeping the TV tuned to election night returns.

Next, we became reindeer road kill (how that

giant sled ran over us without leaving permanent skid marks is beyond me), then toasted time travelers (almost fun . . . except for the smoking hair), and polluted pond scum (which explains the mysterious slime dripping from the people when they exited the ride).

I must say I especially appreciated the attention to wardrobe when we were blundering our way as ballerinas and screaming our lungs out as skydivers. And let's not forget the educational elements while being consumed as afterthought astronauts and human hairballs. Finally, what ride into McDoogle mayhem would be complete without becoming a mixed-up millennium bug that is squashed flatter than a walrus whoopee cushion?

Yes, sir, it was all there. Every highlight (or is it lowlight?) you could imagine (and some you shouldn't). And, as our car shot out of the giant head's ear and came to a stop, I could only do what everyone else was doing—stare in numb astonishment as slime slowly ran down my face.

How is it possible? How can one person possibly live through so much craziness? Even more puzzling, why would people actually pay money to experience such stuff (or read about it!)?

Unfortunately, before I had time to figure out such questions (and maybe solve world hunger while I was at it), my friends, the screaming, hysterical masses, were once again crowding in for a little visit.

"It's him!" they cried as they raced at me. "It's him! It's him! It's him!"

I looked up from the ride and gasped. "It's me! It's me! It's me! It's me!"

The best I figured there were roughly 1,793 of them swarming around the roller coaster. That means 1,793 people who'd all dyed their hair blond, who all wore black-framed glasses, and whose clothes were so dorky that even thrift stores refused to accept them. (Believe me, I've tried.)

Don't get me wrong, it's nice to be loved and adored. But I find it's better to be loved and adored if you're also able to live and breathe. And right now, neither of those two little pastimes seemed possible—not when 1,793 fans are squishing you to death!

"   ," I cried, "   !"

That was supposed to be: *"Mr. Slicko,"* I cried, *"help me!"* But with no air, there were no words. And if I remembered my biology class correctly, no air also means no life.

Now, I hate to complain or be a bad sport, but the last time I talked to my doctor he said dying could be hazardous to my health and that I should avoid it at any cost. Always being one to follow doctor's orders, I did what anyone who hasn't been able to breathe for the last two to three hours would do.

I passed out.

Well, not passed out, really. Just sort of stopped breathing. Which led my heart to sort of stop beating. Which led my life to sort of stop living.

So there I was, crushed to death by 1,788 fans (it would have been 1,793 but one of the girls left for the rest room—and you know girls, if one leaves, four or five gotta follow). Anyway, there I was, undergoing one of my better near-death experiences (it's like anything else, the more you practice the better you get). Anyway, there I was (I'm going to finish this sentence if it kills me. Oh, I guess *it's* too late). Anyway, there I was, getting ready to drop by heaven for a little visit, when I looked down and saw my body with Mr. Slicko on his knees giving me artificial respiration.

The good news was, after a few tries, his mouth-to-mouth resuscitation worked. Before I knew it, my heart was beating and my breath was breathing. The bad news was, Mr. Slicko has definitely got to cut down on eating all those onions. Whew!

A moment later I was staggering back to my feet. And a moment after that, he and the crew were helping me toward the limo. Luckily, the

crowd was no longer a problem since they were
now all busy holding their breath, trying to make
their hearts stop, and pretending to have near-
death experiences. (I guess imitation really is the
sincerest form of flattery.)

"Isn't this incredible!" Mr. Slicko shouted as we
carefully stepped across the 1,788 bodies that were
lying on the ground. "This is going better than
even I had planned!"

"Yeah, right," I gasped, while trying to reset the
various ribs that had been crushed. But even then,
somewhere in the back of my bruised brain, I again
began to suspect that things weren't as right as
they should be.

Little did I realize how right I was in realizing
that right wasn't really that right at all.

Translation: Hang on, sports fans,
          it's gonna get worse . . .

Chapter 7

Reality Pays a Visit

Our limo pulled up to my house and I stepped out, worn and exhausted. (Being incredibly popular can really take a lot out of a guy.)

"We'll see you tomorrow," Mr. Slicko called from the back seat.

"Are we through?" I asked. "Don't you want to keep videotaping?"

"I do," Mr. Slicko said, "but take a look at my crew." He motioned to the sound man, the cameraman, and Lovely Assistant Doris who were all sitting beside him. Each one was still shaking and twitching a little from our last encounter.

"Think they'll be all right?" I asked.

"Sure, they just need a little time off from you, that's all," he said.

"But you're okay?" I asked. "I mean, with all the craziness and chaos and everything?"

"Oh, sure," he said, grinning. "I used to work at Chunky Cheese."

I nodded.

"But we'll be there tomorrow night for the big game," he said.

"Big game?"

"You bet. I promised Coach Kilroy his weight in pretzels if he'd let you play tomorrow."

"Me?" I croaked.

"That's right." He grinned. "And this time you'll have no stunt double. This time you'll be a super-star all on your own."

I did my best to swallow, but my mouth was drier than the Sahara Desert . . . at high noon . . . during a drought.

"So get plenty of rest. We'll see you tomorrow," he said. With that he motioned to the driver, rolled up his window, and the limo pulled away.

I watched as he disappeared. Needless to say, I was pretty nervous. Still, Mr. Slicko had worked everything out so far. I'd already become incredibly famous. And, if he thought I could actually play tomorrow, well then, maybe I really could—

"Wally?"

I turned to see Wall Street heading down the sidewalk. It was great to see my old friend again. Despite our fight yesterday, it felt good to be around somebody who liked me just the way I was, and not because I'd suddenly become superpopular or anything.

"Hey," I smiled.

"Hey," she answered. I could tell something was on her mind. Finally, she spoke. "I just want to let you know I was wrong."

Poor thing. She'd obviously come to apologize. "Don't sweat it," I said and shrugged. "Jealousy can really mess with a person's head."

"What?" she asked.

"I know it's tough not to be envious of someone as popular as I am."

"Wally, that's not what—"

"And, believe me, I certainly understand if being jealous makes you a little, I don't know, 'cranky' sometimes."

"Wally," she angrily cut me off. "I was talking about your toenail clippings collection."

"Oh." I smiled. "So you want to start selling them now?"

She shook her head. "I'm not going to sell them at all."

"What?"

"I'm not going to make money off you pretending to be someone you're not."

I couldn't believe my ears. Wall Street *not* making money off me? Isn't that like water running uphill, or snow in July, or for them to make a TV series about a weird blue dog who gives clues?

"You're not serious." I said.

She nodded. "All of my life I've made money off you. In kindergarten it was selling you bottles of freshly packed dirt . . ."

"From my own back yard," I added.

"In third grade it was left over Kittles and Bits from Collision's cat dish."

". . . and telling me it was a new type of breakfast cereal."

"And last year, charging you for the air you breathed."

"Yeah." I shook my head, chuckling. "But I'm almost caught up on those payments, aren't I?"

She nodded. "Just eleven more to go, Wally. But this . . ." She shook her head. "To make money off you trying to become someone else."

"What are you talking about?" I protested. "The people love me."

"No." She shook her head. "They love the you you're trying to be. Look at you. You're worn out. You're working so hard at being who they want you to be, you've totally forgotten who *you* want *you* to be."

"Hey, that ride back at 2½ Flags is who I am. There were one thousand seven hundred eighty-eight fans all trying to be just like me—well, one thousand seven hundred ninety-three, if you count the ones who had to go to the bathroom."

She shook her head. "That's just an image— that's somebody you're pretending to be. Don't you get it, Wally?"

"That's Willard," I said.

"What?"

"Sorry," I said with a shrug, "force of habit."

"Remember how Pastor Swenson always says that each of us is unique—that there's only one of you and one of me?"

"What's that got to do with—"

"By working so hard to become somebody you're not, you're turning your back on the somebody you were created to be."

"What about all those people falling down at the concert?" I argued. "They were trying to be just like me."

"That's just as bad. You're encouraging *them* to be somebody they're not."

Wall Street was starting to bug me. I'd gone out of my way to still let her be my friend and she was pulling this? Talk about unappreciative. She should be thankful just to be in my presence. She should be grateful that I—

My thoughts were interrupted by Vincent, the mailman. As a postal worker he's been delivering mail on foot for more than twenty years. And believe me, he's got the dog-bite scars to prove it—poodles, Pekinese, pomegranates—you name it, he's been bitten by it. But today he was driving a huge truck.

"Hey, kids!" he shouted.

"What are you doing in that truck?" I yelled.

"Delivering your fan mail."

"My *fan* mail," I said, slowly turning toward Wall Street and throwing her a major smirk. "Did you say *fan* mail?"

"That's right," he said. "There's too much for the mailbox. Where do you want it?"

"Well," I said, still smirking away, "I guess you can drop my *fan* mail at my front door. What do you think, Wall Street? Isn't that where most stars have their *fan* mail delivered?"

"Whatever," she grumbled. "I'm out of here." With that she turned and headed back down the sidewalk.

I couldn't believe what I was seeing. *She* was walking away from *me?* If anything it should be the other way around. But that was okay. If that's how she wanted to be, let her. I had more than enough new friends. Who needed her?

I watched as Vincent backed the truck up our driveway until he was good and close to the front door. Then he pulled a lever and the whole bed of the truck started to rise. Suddenly, I realized what was happening. It was a dump truck! Vincent was delivering my mail in a dump truck!

"No, wait!" I shouted.

As the back end continued to rise, I saw it was completely filled with letters. Millions of them!

"Hold it!" I shouted as I ran toward the back of the truck. "You can't dump them here! Not in front of—"

But that was all I said before the tailgate popped open and the letters began to

tumble
tumble, tumble

out. Before I knew it, I was surrounded by a pile of mail. A pile that just kept growing.

"Vincent, stop!"

But Vincent couldn't hear as they continued to

tumble
tumble, tumble
tumble, tumble, tumble.

Suddenly, I was waist deep, then chest deep, then neck deep. Before I knew it, I was literally drowning in a mountain of mail.

"Vincent, stop!" I choked. "Vincent!"

But he didn't hear me, and the mountain just kept growing.

tumble
tumble, tumble
tumble, tumble, tumble
tumble, tumble, tumble, tumble
tumble, tumble, tumble, tumble, tumble
tumble, tumble, tumble, tumble, tumble, tumble

* * * * *

I'm not sure how long it was before the search-and-rescue team finally saved my life (it's hard to keep track of time when you're unconscious). But by the lack of daylight when they pulled me out, I figured it was sometime in the middle of the night. I tell you, they were a great bunch of guys (and guyettes), and I really appreciated them risking their lives to save mine.

I also appreciated the opportunity to finally *gasp, gasp* breathe fresh air. To finally *hug, hug* feel Mom's arms wrap around me. And to finally hear "Wallace, you know how much this search-and-rescue team is going to cost me?" from Dad.

However, I was not so grateful to see the glaring lights of Mr. Slicko's TV crew or hear his voice shouting, "Look this way, Willard, look this way!"

I turned to him and frowned. "Come on, guys," I complained. "Can't I have a little time alone with my family? I almost died in there."

"I know." Mr. Slicko grinned. "Isn't it cool?"

"Actually, it was pretty painful," I said.

"MY BABY! MY BABY!"

I spun around to see the same actor whose run-away car I'd supposedly saved yesterday and who was wearing the same woman's wig. He/she clutched his/her chest and kept screaming, "My baby! My baby! My poor little poodikins!"

"What's the matter, lady?" one of the search-and-rescue guys shouted.

"My baby's still under there. She's still under those letters!"

His/her acting had not improved since yesterday, and I could tell the search-and-rescue people weren't entirely buying it. But being the heroes they are and figuring it was better to be safe than sorry, they ordered everybody to "stand back, stand back!" And a moment later, they were back to digging.

I could tell they were pretty tired, but they were also very dedicated; so, they kept on pushing themselves to dig and search and dig and search.

"Is there really a baby under there?" I finally asked Mr. Slicko.

"Of course not," he whispered.

"Then why are you making those guys work? Let them rest, they've been at it for hours."

"Are you crazy, Willard? This is your big chance."

"What are you talking about?"

"Just go over to that far side of the pile, way off to the left."

"What's over there?"

"Move a few letters, you'll see."

I glanced back at the search-and-rescue people.

"Go," Slicko whispered. "Go! The sooner you do, the sooner they'll be able to stop."

I gave a reluctant shrug and walked over to the far side of the pile. At the very edge I noticed a few letters moving. I glanced at Slicko, who motioned for me to bend down and investigate.

I stooped over, pushed a handful of letters aside and

"WHAAA!"

sure enough, there was a baby. A baby who had suddenly started

"WHAAAAAAaaa!"

crying its head off.

I quickly scooped the little critter into my arms and stood up just as Slicko's TV crew turned their lights on me.

"You're a hero!" the bad actor cried, as he/she raced to me and nearly knocked me over with his/her hug. "My hero!"

Slicko quickly shoved a microphone in my face. "Tell us, Willard, what does it feel like to save a baby's life?"

I looked up at him, startled. It was obvious he was the one who had planted the baby and even more obvious that he expected me to play along. So I said what any honest, truthful individual would say: "I uh . . ." I cleared my throat. "That is umm . . ."

"Well?" Slicko asked.

"Great!" I suddenly heard myself shout. "It feels great!"

The neighbors and crowd surrounding us began to clap and cheer.

"And that's why *you're* so great!" Mr. Slicko shouted into the mic. "That's why Willard McDorkel has become a hero loved by millions."

I threw a nervous glance over to the search-and-rescue guys—the ones who had just saved my life. They stood quietly in the shadows watching. No one was busy talking to them, no one was busy asking them how they felt. And yet they were the ones who really saved somebody's life. They were the real heroes.

And me . . .

"Come over here to the monitor, Willard." Slicko slapped his hand around my shoulder as he escorted me to it. "Let's take a look at the instant replay of you struggling against all those letters to save that baby's life!"

And me . . .

I was the fake. I was the one pretending to be something I wasn't. It was just like Wall Street had said. I was trying so hard to be somebody I wasn't that I was forgetting who I was.

Unfortunately, it would get worse before it got better. A lot worse . . .

Chapter 8

Blame the Fame

That night I lay in bed unable to sleep. Tomorrow was the basketball game. My big day. Because out there on the basketball court, in front of all my fans, it was just going to be me. No stunt doubles in bad wigs saving runaway cars. No rock and roll bands and special effects making me out to be a superstar. And no finding buried babies to make me out to be a hero.

Tomorrow, I'd be all on my own. Just me.

But the question remained . . . who am "I"? Had I really been working so hard to be what other people wanted me to be that I was no longer being the me *I* wanted to be? Or, more importantly, to be the me God wanted me to be?

With these and about a million other thoughts rattling through my head, I reached for Ol' Betsy. Maybe a good dose of ImaginMan would take

my mind off my problems, because, as I recall, the
poor guy had a few of his own . . .

When we last left our hero, he was
having his brain drained,
  by a video game,
  which was a shame,
  and there was only one person to
  blame—
Hold it a minute! This is no time
for rap music! Not when our hero is busy
falling under the spell of the video
game playing across the side of the Good
Ear Blimp.

"Must . . . find . . . controls," he gasps
as he drops to his hands and knees des-
perately searching for a joystick. "Must
. . . reach . . . next level."

As luck would have it (along with the
usual cool writing on this author's
part), a discarded shopping bag sits
on the curb just ahead. Hoping against
hope, our hero crawls toward it. With
his last ounce of energy, he reaches
inside the bag. But instead of a joystick or remote, there is nothing but
books . . . *Robinson Crusoe, Treasure*

Island, The Adventures of Huckleberry Finn, and, of course, a copy or two of that great American classic series The Incredible Worlds of Wally McDoogle. (Hey, it's my story, I ought to put something in, shouldn't I?)

As he stares at the covers of the books he begins recalling the hours of fun and adventure he had while reading them—the way they unlocked his imagination, the way they made him feel like he was really there. Not like those lame video games where you just press buttons and move controls. No, this was real imagination where he felt what the heroes felt, where he learned what the heroes learned, where he experienced what the heroes experienced.

As he recalls these things, his mind begins to clear. Once again he is able to think and reason—until suddenly a voice blasts out from above,

"Look back up here, ImaginMan."

Jumpin' Jet Planes! It's KidVid's voice! He's been up in the blimp all

along. No wonder ImaginMan couldn't
find his headquarters.

"RESISTANCE IS FUTILE, IMAGINMAN. JOIN
THE MINDLESS MASSES AND LOOK BACK UP
TO MY VIDEO SCREEN."

Using all of his strength, our hero
somehow manages to resist the temptation. He will no longer let his mind
go numb, he will no longer sit and
mindlessly press buttons, he will no
longer—

"RESISTANCE IS FUTILE." The voice
from the blimp grows louder. "JOIN
US, IMAGINMAN. LOOK UP TO THE SKIES
AND TURN YOUR MIND OVER TO ME."

The temptation grows stronger.
ImaginMan grows weaker. "What do I
do?" he cries. "Help me! What do I do?"

"Use your superpowers," I type.

"RESISTANCE IS . . ."

"But what are they? What are my
superpowers?!"

"Your imagination!" I type. "Use your
imagination!"

"That's it?!" ImaginMan cries. "The
only power you've given me is my imagination?!"

"It's one of the greatest powers there is," I type.

BLEEP, PING, BLAM
BLEEP, PING, BLAM

Oh, no! KidVid is trying to seduce our hero by blasting sound effects through the blimp's speakers. Is there no end to his wily wiliness, to his vile villainy, to his lack of good sportsmanship? (And don't even get me started on his table manners.)

Worst of all, it's working!

Soon ImaginMan's eyes glaze over. Soon he starts looking up. Soon his IQ begins dropping. "Must . . . look . . . up. Must reach . . . next—"

"No, ImaginMan!" I frantically type. "Your imagination! Use your imagination!"

"Too much . . . bother. Must reach—"

"No, ImaginMan! Look at those books in your hands. Look at them!"

Using his last ounce of willpower, our hero forces himself to look back down at the books. And that's all it takes. Suddenly, his mind begins to clear.

Suddenly, he remembers how cool it is
to read and to use his imagination.

And, suddenly, he begins putting that
very imagination to use.

In a flash, he races to his Imagin-
Mobile, pulls his trusty ImaginScrew-
driver from the glove compartment, and
begins dismantling his car. Screw by
screw, bolt by bolt, everything comes
apart.

"What are you doing?" I type.

"I'm using my imagination!"

But KidVid refuses to be ignored.
He cranks up the volume until

BLEEP, PING, BLAM
BLEEP, PING, BLAM

the sound effects are deafening.

Still, nothing will stop our hero.
His imagination is in full gear. Soon
he is reassembling the pieces of his
car...but no longer as a car. No, dear
reader, that would be too UNimagi-
native. Instead, he remembers the cre-
ativity of past books, like *The Swiss
Family Robinson*. Instead, he reassem-

bles the pieces of his car into a
giant tower.

It rises higher and higher . . . and
higher some more. In a matter of minutes
it reaches all the way to the blimp.

"Nice work," I type.

But ImaginMan has no time for compli-
ments. Instead, he quickly climbs his
newly created tower, foot by foot, until
he's high enough to leap onto the top
of the blimp. Now if he can just get
inside. Now if he can just stop KidVid.

I took a moment and looked over the story. It
seemed like ImaginMan was finally making some
progress. With a heavy sigh, I reached down, saved
the story, and shut off Ol' Betsy. ImaginMan was
finally on the right track.

I just wished I was.

* * * * *

The following morning Mr. Slicko and his
crew were not downstairs in the kitchen. So, without the TV camera following my brothers' every
move they were back to treating me with their
usual courtesy and respect.

"Hey, Dorkoid, give me that sugar or I'll break your arm." (That, of course, was my sensitive big brother, Burt.)

"Not before he goes to the fridge and grabs me the milk." (Enter my other sensitive big brother, Brock.)

In one way it felt kinda good, sort of like old times. In another way, it made me mad. "Listen," I said, "I don't have to do what you guys say anymore. I'm a big star."

"If you *don't* do what we say, you'll be a *dead* star," growled Burt. (Or was it Brock? I can't always tell their growls apart.)

"That's right," Brock sneered. (Or was it Burt? I have the same problem with their sneers.)

I turned to my father, who sat across the table. In my best whine I cried, "Dad . . ."

And Dad, showing the ultimate care and compassion, came to my defense as best he could. Without a moment's hesitation, he reached out, grabbed the page of the newspaper he was reading, and turned it.

I didn't have to be treated like this. Didn't they know who I was (or pretended I was)? If they didn't, I could think of a million adoring fans who did. A million adoring fans all dying to treat me with the love and respect I deserved.

"Wally," little Carrie asked politely, "could you pass me the cereal?"

"That's it!" I shouted, rising from the table. "I refuse to be treated like everyone's slave!"

Her eyes widened in fear. "I just asked you to pass me the cereal."

"If you knew who I really was, you'd ask to pass *me* the cereal!"

"But"—her little voice started to quiver—"you've already got some."

I glanced down at my bowl. Of course, she was right, but this was no time to be confused with facts. In a huff, I stormed from the room, threw on my jacket, and headed for the door.

"Wally, where are you going?" Mom called from the kitchen.

"I'm going to McArches for breakfast," I said. "I'm going to eat with people who really appreciate me."

"But, Wally—"

"Please"—I turned back to her—"I really need to do this."

"Well, all right," she sighed, "but if you're going out in your pajamas, maybe you should change into those nice Buzz Lightgear ones I gave you for Christmas."

I glanced down at my clothes. Oops. The old Darth Galls I was wearing probably wouldn't cut it. Then again, my Buzz Lightgears were probably not that appropriate, either.

So, after changing into something a little more suitable, I opened our front door, stepped outside, and was met by:

"THERE HE IS!"

"IT'S WILLARD McDORKEL!"

A dozen crazed fans had slept on our porch all night. After the usual screaming and ripping of my clothes, I was finally able to get inside and shut the door.

If I was going out, it was obvious I'd need to wear a disguise. So, with a little help from Carrie, we were able to dress me up like a person who had some sense of fashion. (They'd never recognize me that way.) Unnoticed, I slipped out the back door and in less than fifteen minutes I was over at McArches putting down a few Big Hacks.

I gotta tell you, for the next hour I was in heaven. Not a single person recognized me. I could finally relax. I could finally be myself. *Myself.* I'd almost forgotten how good that was, how good just being me felt.

"Let go of that, it's mine!"

"No, he's mine!"

"Mine!"

"Mom, make him give it back!"

I glanced over at the table beside me. A little boy and his sister were fighting over the latest plastic action figure that McArches was giving away. It was a little blond guy with dark glasses, dressed up in the world's dorkiest clothes.

I couldn't believe it. It was me! The kids were fighting over me!

But, instead of the self-destructo toy Wall Street had shown me earlier, this little action figure jumped and flew and did all sorts of cool stuff. As I watched them continue to fight, I slowly realized another fact. The kids weren't battling over the real me. They were fighting and making a big deal over the make-believe me. The Mr. Slicko version of me.

The thought made me very sad . . . until I remembered tonight's game. Because if I did everything right, if I remembered everything Coach Kilroy had taught me, things would become entirely different. I would no longer be a fake. The clumsy, klutzoid Wally McDoogle would be gone forever. If everything went according to plan, I really could become the ever-popular Willard McDorkel.

If everything went right . . .

Chapter 9

Let the Game Begin

The game wasn't scheduled until 7:00 that evening. Since I had plenty of time, I decided to take the long way home and do some thinking. If things went the way I hoped, this would be my very last day as Wally McDoogle. Finally, in every sense of the word, I'd become Willard McDorkel.

Part of me was excited. And part of me was kind of sad.

So many memories . . . over there was the ice rink where I played my first (and last) hockey game. Just across the street was the baseball field where I visited myself from the future. And, there, high above the city, loomed the reservoir that I actually managed to save while at the same time stopping the city from being flooded. (Hey, even the worst of us can have a good day once in a while.)

Yes, sir, the old Wally McDoogle had really gotten

around. And to be honest, I was going to miss him. Though I doubted I'd miss those wonderful opportunities of being the all-school punching bag and walking disaster area. But still . . .

"Hey, Wally, *munch, crunch*. Wally, is that you?"

I recognized the voice before I even turned around. (Then, of course, there was that delightful aroma of potato, corn, and taco chip breath.)

"Hey, Opera," I said.

"What are you all *crunch, munch* dressed up for?"

"Oh, this," I said, referring to my disguise. "It's so I won't be recognized by all my fans. What's up?"

"Not *munch, munch* much. Guess you're waiting for the big game tonight."

"Yeah." I nodded. "With any luck I'll finally become the Willard McDorkel everybody thinks I am."

"The one everybody loves and adores," he said.

"That's right," I agreed.

"Belch." He nodded.

A long moment of silence grew between us. (Well, as much silence as you can have over rattling chip bags, continual crunching, and occasional—)

"BURPs!" Finally, he spoke. "Wally?"

"Yeah."

"Wall Street and me, we've been talking."

Oh, brother, I thought, *more complaining.* Since Wall Street was no longer speaking to me, it looked like she was now sending her lectures courtesy of Opera Express.

"Listen," I said, "if you're going to give me a speech about how I should be myself, then you can—"

"No, actually, we decided just the opposite."

"Opposite?" I asked.

"We think we were wrong."

"Wall Street, too?" I asked.

"Belch," he added with a nod.

I couldn't believe my ears (or his breath). Was it possible? Had Wall Street really admitted she was wrong?

I waited patiently for more information. But Opera was in no hurry. Instead, he finished his bag of chips, tossed it aside in the nearest trash receptacle, then pulled up his shirt and ripped off the emergency reserve bag taped to his chest.

The silence was killing me. Finally, I asked, "What do you mean, 'wrong'? How were you guys wrong?"

"If *crunch, crunch* you want to be somebody else, who are we to stop you?"

"You really mean that?" I asked.

"Sure, if you want to give up the old Wally McDoogle to become famous and popular, that should be your decision, not ours."

I nodded, grateful that they were finally seeing things my way.

"As long as it's what *you* want," he added.

"Of course it is," I said. "Who else would there be?"

He gave a shrug, tossed in another handful of chips. "Mmour famms," he said, "miffer miffwoh."

"Pardon me?"

He swallowed and tried again. "Your fans. Mr. Slicko. If you're making the change 'cause you want to, that's cool. If you're making it 'cause they want you to, that's not so cool."

I nodded slowly, giving it some thought.

"Well—*burp*—whatever you decide. We just wanted you to know we're behind you."

"Does that mean you're going to the game tonight?"

"Hey"—he smiled, showing a good two-day build-up of chips on his teeth—"what are friends for?"

With that he slapped me on the back, let out another belch for good measure, and started down the street. I stood there watching after him. Opera didn't talk much (since talking usually interferes with eating), but when he did speak, it was often something important—something like this. And the more I thought of his words, the more right I knew he was. It was okay to change . . . as long as it was what *I* wanted to do. Not so I could keep a million fans loving me, not so I could keep Mr. Ricko Slicko happy, but because I wanted to.

I turned and headed for home. But I couldn't

shake the question. It kept rattling around in the back of my head for the rest of the afternoon . . . and as I prepared for the game.

Who did I really want to change for? Them? . . . Or me?

* * * * *

Later that evening we were in the middle of the big game. The gym was packed with screaming fans and our team was winning in a major sort of way. Very major.

"Way to go, Clams!" Coach Kilroy shouted and clapped as we scored point after point after point. "Way to go!"

It was a massacre. The first half wasn't even over, and we were already ahead by fifty points! That's fifty as in *50*! I couldn't believe it. In fact, we were so far ahead that Coach had already sent in the scrubs and subs. That meant even the worst players were getting a chance to play. Well, all the worst players but me. For some reason Coach thought it safer to keep me on the bench.

The game continued as one of our scrubs, Pee Wee Halfpintser, stole the ball. He dribbled down court, faked to his left, then went up for a perfect lay-up. (The fact that he was three feet tall and needed a stepladder just to tie his shoes made the feat all the more impressive.) The crowd went wild, clapping and cheering and hooting.

Yes, sir, everyone was having a great time . . . except Mr. Slicko. The poor guy was sitting in the stands behind us, fuming in a Mount Saint Helens kind of way. And for good reason. He and his TV crew had come specifically to videotape me playing. And so far they'd only videotaped me sitting.

Earlier, I thought he was going to blow a gasket when he came down from the stands and got into Coach's face. "Why aren't you letting Willard play?" he shouted. "We had a deal! You're supposed to let him play!"

But Coach had shaken his head and answered, "I said he could play only when it was safe."

"You're fifty points ahead, what could be safer?" Slicko shouted.

Coach tossed me a quick look and answered. "With his skills and natural athletic ability . . . I'm waiting till we clear a hundred."

Soon the halftime buzzer sounded, and we all leaped to our feet and headed to the locker room. The score read:

HOME	63
VISITORS	**14**

I don't want to sound overconfident or anything, but it sure looked like we had this one in
the bag.

Down in the locker room we all took a seat as
Coach Kilroy entered grinning from ear to ear. "You
guys are terrific!" he shouted. "Unbelievable!"

Everyone clapped and cheered. Figuring now
was as good a time as any, I raised my hand.

"Yeah, McDoogle."

"Do you think I'll get a chance to play?"

Instantly, the team grew quiet. A couple stole
uneasy glances at each other. Pee Wee coughed
nervously.

Finally, Coach answered. "Maybe, McDoogle,
but no promises."

"But I really want to help out the team," I said.

Pencil Lead (who was a scrub and got his nick-
name from being six-foot-seven and weighing
eighty-two pounds) answered, "You're helping
us by doing just what you're doing."

"That's right," Pee Wee answered, his voice
slightly higher than fingernails on a blackboard.
"We need somebody to keep that bench nice and
warm when we take a break and sit down."

"Come on," I argued. "I really want to help."

"All right," Coach said, "I've got something for
you."

"You do?" I asked hopefully.

"Yeah, go to the dryer behind these lockers and get the boys some clean towels. They've worked up quite a sweat."

I knew he was just trying to get rid of me, but that was okay. At least it was something. I got up, headed behind the wall of lockers, and opened the door to the giant dryer. I pulled out a bunch of fresh towels and started dumping them into the giant laundry basket. But there were more than I expected and to get them all in I had to lean into the basket and smash some down. At least, leaning into the basket and smashing some down was what I had in mind.

Unfortunately, my great coordination had other ideas . . .

First, there was the problem of leaning into the basket. Actually, I had to give a little jump to do it. No problem, except my little jump was just a little too clumsy . . . which sent me flying head-first into the basket just a little too hard. Even that wouldn't have been a problem if the laundry basket didn't have wheels. But, of course, it did. It took off like a rocket!

"MAUGH! . . ."
(It would have been
"AUGH!" but it's hard yelling
with a face full of towels.)

I'm not sure what the speed limit is inside the boys' locker room, but I wish somebody would have pulled me over and given me a ticket. Unfortunately, there was no one to stop me but

K-THUD

that wall of lockers. It stopped me all right, but not before teetering back and forth and back and forth and—

"Look out!" Coach Kilroy yelled. "The lockers are coming down!"

Before the team could scramble out of the way, the entire wall of lockers tumbled and fell . . . right on top of them.

K-RASH
K-sprain
K-break
K-you-name-it and it was injured.

During the collision my laundry cart tipped over and threw me out. I staggered to my feet and quickly ran to the other side to check out the damage.

It was worse than I feared. On the McDoogle Scale of Mishaps it rated an 11.2. Where my team-mates had once been sitting, there was now a giant mountain of lockers. In fact, the entire team had been buried in a Pompeii kind of way. And if it wasn't for the occasional arm or leg sticking out, it would have been impossible to tell that anyone was there. (Well, except for the groaning. There was lots and lots of groaning.)

I'll save you the gory details. Let's just say that after the paramedics pulled the guys out and started setting their broken body parts, there were only four players in good enough shape to play . . . Pee Wee Halfpintser, Pencil Lead, and a couple of others.

It was about this time that the buzzer in the gymnasium sounded. Halftime was over and the third quarter was about to begin.

"Oh, no," Pee Wee squeaked. "We'll have to forfeit."

"Never," Coach called as he lifted up his bandaged head from the stretcher.

"What do you mean?" Pencil Lead croaked. "There are only four of us."

But Coach, who had obviously watched one too many showings of *Saving Private Ryan,* shouted, "I don't care if there's only one of you. We've got a job to do, so let's go back out there and do it! Do you hear me, men? Let's go back out there and win, win, win!"

With those stirring words of inspiration (no doubt

spoken from a state of delirium) all four of the
team members raced for the stairs, shouting and
pumping themselves up with such battle cries as,
"We're dead! We're goners! I want my mommy!"

But as I followed them up the stairs it became
obvious what had just happened. My big chance
had finally arrived. As they headed onto the floor
to face off for the tipoff, I joined them.

"Wally, what are you doing?" Pee Wee squeaked
as we took our position around the center circle.

I motioned to the rest of the team. "There's only
four of you."

"Yeah."

"And it takes five to make a team."

"Ah." Pee Wee nodded. "Well listen, that's awfully
thoughtful and everything. But after watching you
at practice the last couple of days . . ."

"Yeah?"

He scrunched up his face, trying to find the right
words.

Pencil Lead leaned down and helped out. "It
would be better for us if you don't play."

"What's that?" one of the referees asked.

Pee Wee swallowed. "We were just telling Wally
here—"

"I know what you were telling him, son. But the
rules call for five players on a team."

"Well, yeah, but . . ." Pee Wee pointed helplessly to me. "I mean, look at him."

The referee turned to me, took a long gander, then sadly nodded. "I see your point, but rules are rules. Either he plays or you forfeit."

Pee Wee and Pencil Lead looked hard at each other, obviously trying to figure out which was worse, forfeiting or letting me play.

"Well?" the ref asked.

After a deep breath, Pee Wee finally squeaked, "Okay, he plays."

My heart leaped. Of course, it would have leaped a bit more if he hadn't stood on his tiptoes and whispered into my ear, "Just don't touch the ball, okay?"

I nodded. "I'll do my best."

"That's what we're worried about," Pencil Lead sighed. "That's exactly why we're worried."

Chapter 10

Wrapping Up

Pencil Lead and his opponent lined up for the tipoff. The ref threw the ball up and Pencil Lead easily outjumped his man (not that you have to do a lot of jumping when you're six-foot-seven). Unfortunately, his coordination hadn't quite caught up with his height, which explains why he missed the ball completely and landed on his rear. (It also explains why he was on the scrub team.)

But not to worry, the guy I was supposed to guard got the ball and raced downcourt.

"That's your man!" Pee Wee squeaked. "That's your man!"

"I know." I beamed just as the guy went in for an easy two-point lay-up. "Isn't he great? I'm so happy for him!"

"You're not supposed to be happy for him, you're supposed to stop him!"

"I am?"

Once again, I'll save you the gory details. Let's just say that's how our defense went the rest of the game (which explains why they racked up points faster than my big brothers collect speeding tickets).

Unfortunately, our offense was no better. Since I'd been given strict orders not to go near the ball, it meant their team had five players against our four. No problem, except that it meant their guys could double-team our guys whenever they wanted—which was all the time!

This would explain why, by the end of the third quarter, they'd scored over thirty points and we'd scored a grand total of . . . zero.

Yes, sir, we were giving new meaning to the word *pathetic*. (It was a good thing you couldn't subtract points or we would have really been in trouble.) I suspected things weren't going exactly the way Mr. Slicko had hoped, either. And when I glanced into the stands and saw him shaking his head and bawling like a baby, I knew I was right.

And still we continued to play (if you could call it that). Our score remained frozen at a respectable, tried-and-true 63 (Hey, if you find a good thing, why change it?), while the other team steadily gained on us. On and on it went. And then, on some more. By the time we got down to one minute left in the game, they'd scored a total of 58 points.

Uh-oh.

At thirty seconds they were up to 62 points.

Double uh-oh.

That's when Pee Wee called time-out and we huddled together.

"Okay, guys," his little voice squeaked. "We've got thirty seconds left. We're ahead by one point. If we hang on, we can still win this thing."

Everyone nodded.

"Just don't do anything stupid."

Again we nodded.

"And Wally?"

"I know, I know," I said, "just stay out of the way."

"Now you're getting it," he said, grinning. "We can win this thing if we keep our heads." With that we broke and raced back onto the floor. Pencil Lead tossed the ball to Pee Wee, who immediately dribbled downcourt.

I glanced at the clock. It read:

25 seconds.

Pee Wee faked to the left, then tried to fire off a long shot. But with his man and my man both covering him, it was more like a suicide mission. The ball missed the rim completely, bounced off the backboard, and came sailing toward me.

Triple uh-oh!

At first I thought of doing the smart thing and leaping out of the way. But that's not what the great Willard McDorkel would do. No, he'd catch the ball and save the day. So, it was obvious, I had no choice. I had to catch it.

Fortunately, all my training from the last two days paid off and, wonder of wonders, I actually caught the thing. Suddenly, two guys were all over me trying to get it. I had to act fast. I had to pass to somebody in the open.

Then I spotted him. A person totally in the clear. I fired the ball to him. The good news was, it was a perfect pass. The bad news was, it was to the wrong team. (Hey, you can't have everything.) He caught the ball and broke downcourt to score two more points.

I looked up at the scoreboard. It read:

```
HOME 63
VISITORS 64
```

For the first time in the game we were behind. We were down by one point with only sixteen seconds left on the clock. But it wasn't over yet. We still had time to make a basket.

Pee Wee tossed the ball inbounds to Pencil Lead. But he only got halfway downcourt before he was double-teamed and had the ball stolen. Then, the weirdest thing happened. Instead of racing downcourt to try to score two more points, their player spun around, spotted me, and tossed me the ball.

"What are you doing?" I cried.

He shrugged. "You're the best player we've got. If anybody can score us another point or two, I figure it's you."

Needless to say, his comment made me mad. Not only was it mean and insensitive, it was probably the truth. But I'd show him. Instead of doing something with the ball (Translation: Helping our opponents), I'd do absolutely nothing with it. I'd just hold it until time ran out. At least that way, it would be nice and safe and we'd only lose by one point.

But Pee Wee didn't appreciate my plan. "Pass it," he kept squeaking. "We've got ten seconds left. Pass it! Pass it!"

But I wasn't falling for that old trick, no, sir. No way was I going to help the other side score any more points.

"Wally!" Now Pencil Lead was running toward me. "Wally, give me the ball!"

I shook my head. No, sir, I'd done enough damage already. I couldn't pass, I couldn't dribble, so

I'd do the only thing I knew how to. I'd cling to the ball with all my might.

The crowd started to boo.

"Wally," Pencil Lead yelled, "we've only got eight seconds!"

I clung to the ball tighter.

He tried to take it from me, but my grip was like iron. In fact, I wrapped my whole body around it and dropped to the floor. For some reason the crowd appreciated this even less, but there was no way I was giving up that ball.

In desperation, Pencil Lead acted. It wasn't his best idea, but it was his only one. The big guy reached down and picked up the ball . . . and me!

"This is your last chance, Wally. Let go!"

I shook my head.

"All right," he said. "Then hang on real tight."

He stood up, and to the crowd's astonishment (let alone mine) he began dribbling the ball with me still attached.

K-Bounce "OW!"
K-Bounce "OW!"

It was quite a ride. And over the sound of my breaking ribs, I could hear the crowd cheering and counting down as the seconds clicked off: "Five, four . . ."

K-Bounce "OW!"
K-Bounce "OW!"

We continued moving downcourt.

"Three, two . . ."

"SHOOT!" Pee Wee's voice screeched. "SHOOT!"

"One . . ." And then it happened. Suddenly, the ball and I were sailing high through the air. Actually, the view wasn't half bad. On the court below, I could see Pee Wee and Pencil Lead standing with their mouths open. Over in the stands, I could see Mr. Slicko and his TV crew busy videotaping. And there, not too far from the approaching basket, stood my old friends Wall Street and Opera.

It was a beautiful moment. No longer was I the great Willard McDorkel, no longer was I being something I wasn't. Instead, it was just me, Wally McDoogle, doing what I do best.

Talk about exhilarating, talk about a great feeling. Who cared what the crowd thought? Who cared what my fans felt? It was terrific just to be me again. Unfortunately, what was not so terrific was hitting the backboard so hard that it shattered into a gazillion pieces.

Yet, over the roaring crowd and shattering backboard (not to mention my shattering head), I heard Wall Street shout, "Stick out your arms, Wally! Stick out your arms!"

It was great having her talk to me again, just like old times. And since I had nothing else better to do, I decided to take her advice. I stuck the ball out over my head just in time to feel it and my hands go shooting through the net, followed by my head and chest . . . just as the buzzer sounded to end the game.

The crowd went wild. And, hanging in the net by my feet, I managed to turn and see the scoreboard. It read:

```
┌─────────────────────────┐
│    HOME 65              │
│    VISITORS 64         │
└─────────────────────────┘
```

I couldn't believe it! Somehow, someway (but in true McDoogle style), we had won! It was a little too close and a lot too embarrassing, but we had won! It was a little too painful, but we had won! Of course, I'd have loved to stick around and join in the celebration, but with all the bouncing and backboard shattering going on I had something more pressing to do . . .

Like drop into major unconsciousness.

* * * * *

The first people I saw when I came to were Opera

and Wall Street. They were hovering over me as the paramedics carried me toward the ambulance. "Nice work, Wally!" Wall Street shouted over the commotion. "It's great to have you back!"

"Burp." Opera nodded.

I wanted to say something, to agree with them, to tell them how good it felt, but it's hard to speak when your jaw is broken in seventeen places. Yet I managed to nod, even give a little smile.

"Step aside!" Mr. Slicko shouted. "Step aside!" Suddenly, he was looking down at me. "Don't worry about a thing, Willard. I can fix it in the editing. If we cut out all your klutziness and add lots of computerized special effects, you won't look like a total idiot. I'm sure I'll be able to save your reputation."

Again I tried to speak, and this time I got out a word. Actually two: "Monnn't mahver."

"What?" Mr. Slicko leaned closer. "What did you say?"

I tried again, this time speaking as clearly as possible: "Don't bother."

* * * * *

Yes, sir, it felt great to be back to my old self again. Of course, everybody made plenty of jokes about my performance (or lack of it), and of

course Coach was charging my folks for destroy-
ing the backboard, the locker room, as well as
making us pay his psychiatric bills. (Actually, we
were still paying for those from his last encounter
with me.) But all of this was pretty normal for me.
Maybe not for the great Willard McDorkel, but
definitely for the not-so-great, somewhat average
Wally McDoogle. The Wally McDoogle that I liked
being and planned on remaining.

And Ricko Slicko? He and Lovely Assistant Doris
headed back to New York where he's still running
his advertising company. The last I heard he was
going to relax for a while and take on something
easier—like trying to elect Cruella De Vil president of the Society for the Prevention of Cruelty
to Animals.

And my superhero story? Well, by the time I got
around to finishing it (after all the bones in my
arms and hands were healed), it read something
like this:

When we last left our hero, he had
leaped atop the Good Ear Blimp that
KidVid has stolen to rule the world.
Now, running along the top of the blimp,
he looks for some way to enter the
fanatical fiend's hijacked headquarters.

But alas and alack (whatever that
means), the surface of the blimp is
as smooth as Brock's face (even though
he keeps saying he has to shave). The
only thing visible is a door with a
sign that reads:

ENTER HERE FOR
FANATICAL FIEND'S HIJACKED
HEADQUARTERS

It's a long shot, but with nothing
else to go on, ImaginMan gives it a
try. He opens the door, climbs down the
ladder, and voilà (I found that in the
same dictionary as alas and alack),
there is KidVid! He stands alone in his
giant room switching switches, dialing
dials, and, er . . . knobbing knobs.

"KidVid!" our hero shouts.

The awfully antagonistic alien alters
his attention. (Translation: He turns
around.)

"ImaginMan!" he gasps. "How did you
get up here? How did you find me?"

"That's easy," our hero boasts, "I

just, uh . . . that is . . ." He scratches
his head trying to remember.

"You used your imagination," I type.

"I just used my imagination," he
shouts. "And, uh . . . er . . ."

"And read your sign," I type.

"And read your sign." (Just 'cause
the guy's a superhero doesn't make him
a supergenius.)

"AND WHAT ARE YOU GOING TO DO NOW?"
the bad guy taunts. "TRY TO SHUT ME
DOWN?"

"Well," our hero replies, "now that
you bring it up . . ."

"FIRST, WHY NOT SIT BESIDE ME AND
PLAY A VIDEO GAME?"

"I'd love to, but I have to find your
main power supply to shut you down."

"ARE YOU SURE?" KidVid reaches
over and with one flick of the switch

> *BLEEP, PING, BLAM*
> *BLEEP, PING, BLAM*

they are suddenly surrounded by the
sound of a video game. Then, even more
suddenly-ier (don't try that spelling
at home, kids) the entire inside of

the blimp turns into one giant DVD
screen.

"Look up!" KidVid shouts. "Look
around you! Look at the screen!"

The temptation is strong, but
ImaginMan finds a way to resist. He
begins imagining he is one of those
cool heroes he's read about (no doubt
in one of those cool *My Life As . . .*
novels). He remembers the different
ways the different heroes were able to
overcome their temptations and beat the
bad guys. It's tough, but by practic-
ing what he's read, ImaginMan is able
to keep his eyes off the screen until,
Eureka! (Yup, that's in the same dictionary) he spots another sign that
reads:

> *WARNING:*
> *MAIN POWER PLUG!*
> *PULL ONLY TO SHUT OFF POWER*
> *AND END STORY!*

In a burst of inspiration, he races to
the plug and wraps both hands around it.

"No, NOT THAT!" KidVid cries. "DON'T PULL THAT!"

"Your days are over, KidVid," our hero shouts as the good-guy music begins to play softly in the background. "No longer will you enslave my world with your video games."

"BUT THEY'RE SO MUCH FUN," KidVid whines. "EVERYONE MUST PLAY THEM."

"That's where you are wrong, my fiendish little friend." The music grows louder as our hero places his hands on his hips and the wind begins blowing his cape. "Each of us must choose for ourselves. For those who want to play video games, let them play. For those who want to use their minds and imaginations, let them use their minds and imaginations."

"OH, NO," KidVid groans. "HAVE WE ALREADY COME TO THE PART OF THE STORY WHERE THE HERO GIVES HIS SPEECH?"

ImaginMan grins. "That's right. You see, each of us has been created uniquely. And to really be happy each of us must become the best 'us' we can be. For some it may be playing video games, for others it may be wearing these stupid capes and saving the world."

"OR FOR OTHERS," KidVid adds, "IT CAN BE WRITING THESE WHACKED-OUT STO-RIES WITH THESE SYRUPY ENDINGS."

"Hey!" I type. "Watch it!"

Our hero continues as the music grows louder. "Each of us has been uniquely created by God. And each of us should be allowed to become who we are—not what others want us to be."

"I UNDERSTAND," KidVid cries. "SUDDENLY, EVERYTHING YOU SAY MAKES SENSE!"

"Of course it does," ImaginMan says with a grin. "After all, we've only got a few more lines left in the story. Listen, to prove to the readers out there that you really do understand, that you really have changed, why don't you give me a hand with pulling this giant plug?"

"HEY, THAT'S A SUPERSWELL IDEA," KidVid says as he heads over to join our hero at the giant outlet. "THEN MAYBE YOU CAN SHOW ME SOME OF THE NIFTY KEEN THINGS YOU DO IN YOUR LIFE, AND I'LL SHOW YOU WHAT I DO IN MINE."

"Neato," ImaginMan cries, "that would be just so superswell."

And so, the archenemies work together to disconnect the power to KidVid's video machine. Once again the human race can make their own decisions, once again they will have free will, and once again they have the chance to become the special individuals each of them was created to be.

I reread the ending one last time. It was so sugary sweet that it was a three- maybe even four-cavity ending. But I had definitely gotten my point across. And, as I sat there staring at the screen, waiting for the next McDoogle mishap to strike, I could rest assured that it would at least be *my* disaster, that it would be *my* custom-designed catastrophe and nobody else's. Because just as there's only one KidVid, one ImaginMan, and one of you . . . there's only one Wally-the-Walking-Disaster-Area McDoogle!

And for that, I guess, we can all be thankful.